Creepy Classics
Ghost Stories from Ancient Rome

Juliette Harrisson

CREEPY CLASSICS: GHOST STORIES FROM ANCIENT ROME

Copyright © Juliette Harrisson 2024

All rights reserved. No part of this publication may be reproduced, transmitted, or stored in a retrieval system in any form or by any means without permission in writing from the copyright owner, nor otherwise circulated in any form of binding or cover other than that in which it is published and without a similar condition being imposed on the subsequent purchaser.

Cover illustration by Sam Basnett
Cover designed using Canva Pro

ISBN-13 : 979-8340129956

DEDICATION

For John – it's all for you

CONTENTS

Acknowledgments	i
One Cheap Summer Sandal	1
The Haunted House	11
Under the Kitchen Floor	21
The Dead Marriage	32
A Warning	40
A Spanish Werewolf in Rome	48
A Tomb for a Wedding-Bed	56
The Witch of Thessaly	66
The Fault in Ourselves	75
Of Blood and Gods	83
Home	94
A Tortured Soul	105
Dies Irae	115
Author's notes	128
About the Author	142

ACKNOWLEDGMENTS

This book would not have been possible without the support of my husband, Justin. Thank you for all you do for us, we don't deserve you.

Thanks also to all my friends, students, and colleagues who have talked to me about ghost stories over the years! Particular thanks go to Tony Keen and Liz Gloyn for requesting Pliny's haunted house and Petronius' werewolf stories (respectively) when they kindly appeared as guests on my Creepy Classics podcast.

ONE CHEAP SUMMER SANDAL

Inspired by Cicero, *On Divination*, 1.57 and Valerius
Maximus, *Memorable Deeds and Sayings*, 1.7ext.10

Some years ago I was travelling from Rome to Athens with a dear friend of mine, Decimus. We took a ship to Corinth and then walked from there, taking our time to talk, to enjoy the Greek countryside, and to try out some of the local wines. The day it happened, we were somewhere in the countryside around Megara. The olive groves were flowering, the sun was shining and the roads were peaceful, but after a couple of weeks of travelling together, tempers were starting to get frayed despite our idyllic surroundings.

"Quintus, hold up – I've got another stone in my bloody sandal!" complained Decimus, stopping by the side of the road to shake out his shoe. It was a rather cheap light summer sandal. He never took much care of his appearance, Decimus.

"I'm getting hot," I said, rubbing my neck and squinting against the sun. It was mid-afternoon. "Do you think we'll make it as far as Megara today?"

"Maybe, but do we want to?" Decimus squished his sweaty foot back into his sandal with a squeak. 'Didn't you say you have a cousin who lives around here? Could we stay with him?"

"That's true – yes, I'm sure Aristo would be happy to have us," I replied. "His home is a bit small, but he might be able to squeeze us all in, just about." I gestured towards the four of us – Decimus, myself, and our two slaves, Xanthias (Decimus's) and Nicias (mine). "I believe he has a daughter who may be ready for marriage soon, too." I attempted a wink, but it went a bit wrong and turned into blinking against the sun again.

"Sounds good," said Decimus with a grin. He looked ahead along the road. "Look, there's a sign pointing to a taverna just up the road. Let's stop for a drink and cool off, then carry on to your cousin's for the evening."

"I'm not sure," I said slowly. "If we're going to impose on Aristo for dinner, not to mention finding space for all of us to stay, I think we should get ourselves over there earlier rather than later. We should keep on going, and rest when we reach his house."

"Oh come on, I want a drink!" complained Decimus. "When in Greece, drink where the Greeks do!" He looked so grumpy, I gave in and we headed down a small path that branched off from the main road towards the taverna.

The taverna was a small, shabby-looking building half-hidden behind a grove of trees. A few desultory seats were placed outside, but most of the clientele seemed to be inside the rather dingy main room, drinking silently. I disliked it immediately – though of course, having not wanted to stop there, I was already in a mood to find fault with it. But it was really helping my case. It smelled funny, too.

"This place is *nasty*, Decimus," I muttered to him as quietly as possible. "It's the sort of place I'm not convinced they even bother to wash the cups. Let's just carry on to Aristo's."

"I am really fed up of walking and my foot is properly starting to hurt now," objected Decimus, pointedly rubbing his foot to demonstrate. "I just want to stop for one drink, come on!"

Grumbling, I agreed, and we took a small table as near to the door as possible. Nicias and Xanthias stood nearby, hunched against the dirty walls, making faces when they thought we weren't looking.

We both ordered a cup of wine. When the server – who

appeared to be the owner – brought it over, he looked us up and down in a way that was frankly creepy, taking in our rings, our shoes, and the two slaves trying hard not to touch the wall.

"You travelling, gents?" he asked, and his breath stank.

"Yes, all the way from Rome to Athens," said Decimus cheerfully, before I could send the man away without giving him any personal details.

"Aah, you don't know the area, then?" said the man. "Or anyone around here?"

"No, I don't," Decimus continued while I tried to kick him under the table to make him stop. "I've never been here before. It's a pretty place." He looked at me as if expecting me to mention Aristo, but I had no intention of prolonging a conversation with the slimy innkeeper and stayed stubbornly silent.

"It is, it is," agreed the taverna owner, though his face looked like he didn't approve. He squinted at us. "You must be tired," he said, "after all that travelling. We do rooms as well – why don't you put up here for the night? You can enjoy the local scenery for a while, and start fresh tomorrow."

"No, thank you," I said as politely as I could. I opened my mouth and drew breath to add that my cousin would be taking care of us for the night, but before I could speak, Decimus talked over me and announced, "what a good idea!"

"Let's talk about it," I said through gritted teeth. "Thank you," I added to the greasy man, in a tone that clearly said, 'go away'.

"What's the matter with you?" Decimus demanded as soon as the man had turned away. "You kept saying your cousin doesn't really have room for all of us, so why don't we just stay here?"

"Decimus, this place is a shithole!" I exclaimed. "And I'd like to see Aristo anyway. His place is only a couple of hours' walk away, and it's still afternoon. There's no reason we shouldn't carry on – and if you're very lucky, you might catch a glimpse of his daughter." I waggled my eyebrows suggestively, trying to sweeten my voice and the deal with it.

But Decimus had barely heard that last part.

"A couple of hours! Do you know what that will do to my foot?" he objected.

"There's nothing wrong with your foot!" I said.

"Yes there is! That stupid stone gave me a cramp, and I don't think this sandal fits properly," he said.

"We'll get you new sandals tomorrow," I told him. "In the meantime, Nicias gives a pretty good foot massage, how about you let him have a look, see if he can get you up and moving again long enough to get to Aristo's?"

Decimus sulked, but he could not think of a reason to refuse. "Fine," he said, taking off his sandal and holding out his foot for Nicias, who bent down and got to work. We sat in silence, and I started to gulp down my wine as quickly as possible, so we could get out of there. It tasted sour.

Things seemed to be going well enough for a few minutes, but then Decimus lent over to grab a bowl of figs from a nearby table. The sudden motion knocked Nicias off balance and he sat down hard on Decimus's discarded shoe.

"Hey!" cried Decimus, looking up in anger. "Watch out for my stuff you clumsy idiot!" And with that, he boxed Nicias' ears, hard.

"Hey!" I shouted back at him. "It wasn't his fault, you hate those shoes anyway, and I'll thank you not to attack my slave please!"

"Oh calm down, I haven't hurt him, and I'll pay you if I have," said Decimus.

"That's not the point!" I cried. "Nicias did nothing wrong, and even if he had, he's my slave and it's none of your business to punish him."

"Well, tell your stupid slave not to damage my things! Look at this sandal," and Decimus held the item up for inspection. "I have to wear this into town before I can buy more, and look at it, it's ruined!" He waved it about so roughly that the bent shape of the shoe started to creak and break. "Your slave damaged my property, and I don't see why

I shouldn't discipline him for it since you obviously don't do so often enough!" And with that, he hit Nicias hard across the ribs with the now very broken sandal.

I stood up, in a state of cold fury now. "That's it," I said through clenched teeth. "I don't know what's got into you today, but I've had enough. Forget coming with me to Aristo's – you can stay here if you like it so much. There isn't room for you anyway. I'm going to see my cousin, who serves *good* wine," – I threw the dregs of my cup in his face, for extra effect – "and I'll see you in the agora in Megara tomorrow evening." Without waiting for a reply, I nodded my head towards Nicias (who was cradling his bruised side) and we strode out of the door. I saw Xanthias looking miserably at the grimy taverna as we headed out, but I didn't look back to Decimus. I stomped out of the door without turning around and marched away.

*****

Although the evening walk was tiring, once I got to Aristo's, I had a very pleasant evening. He was impressively unflustered at my sudden and rather late arrival and happily put me up in his small spare room, with Nicias on the floor at my feet. I even caught a glimpse of his daughter, though she was too young to be seriously considered just yet.

After a very pleasant dinner accompanied by much better wine than the taverna's barrel scrapings, I retired to my room and settled into Aristo's very comfortable guest bed. Good food, good wine, and considerably less grumpy company soon sent me into a deep, restful sleep.

It must have been well after midnight when I found myself in the grip of a truly unpleasant dream. I have always been lucky that I do not get nightmares very often, but when I do get them, I find them particularly disturbing, perhaps because they're so unusual for me. So this one made quite an impression.

I had been dreaming quite peacefully of a quiet beach I

knew of down in the bay near Pompeii, waves lapping up against the shore while I lay back on an expanse of soft white sand and looked up at the sky in contentment. But suddenly, the face of Decimus rose up in front of my eyes, blocking the dream-sun. He looked terrible, and terrifying. His familiar features were contorted by some kind of extreme emotion – perhaps severe panic, or fear, or even anger. One eye bulged and the skin around it was black, one tooth was missing, and there were specks of blood dashed across his cheeks.

"Quintus! Quintus!" he called out my name, and his voice was strained and rasping. "Save me! Quintus, the owner of the taverna is trying to kill me! He's already stolen my money and he wants my rings as well! I've managed to shut him out but the door won't hold! You have to come help me! Save me! Save me Quintus!"

His face was transparent against my idyllic beach scene, but I could make out the shadow of Xanthias' body slumped against a door behind him and I could hear the echoes of someone banging on it from outside. "Help me!" he cried one more time, before I tumbled out of bed in fright and woke up.

I had fallen more or less on top of Nicias, who woke up with a start, so by the time we had stumbled out into the main room to see if there was any wine left, the whole household was awake. Aristo came to find out what was wrong.

"I have to go, Aristo!" I cried. "I just had the most awful dream – Decimus is in terrible trouble! That horrible greasy innkeeper is trying to kill him! I have to get back to that taverna and save him!"

"What?" said Aristo, calling for the wine from a bleary-eyed slave. "Why on earth would an innkeeper want to kill your friend?"

"He's trying to steal his rings!" I said, aware as I said it that this was possibly not the most compelling reason for a murder. "Besides, I think the man's a brute, he probably *likes* killing."

"Don't be daft," said Aristo calmly, handing me a cup of wine. "Don't you think if one of the local innkeepers was a killer, we'd know about it?"

"Not necessarily – not if he targets strangers," I pointed out, though the edge was starting to wear off my panic.

"Okay, okay," said Aristo gently. "But you said the taverna was a couple of hours' walk away – if he's attacking your friend right now, wouldn't it be too late by the time you got there?"

"I don't know," I shrugged. "I could run. He's barred the door for the moment. If it holds out a little longer, I could probably get there. At the very least, I could try."

Aristo rubbed his tired eyes and sighed. "If you really want to, I won't stop you, of course," he said. "But Quintus, I honestly think you're over-reacting – it was just a dream. Has anything you've dreamed about ever really happened? I mean, last week I dreamed that all my teeth fell out, but look – they're all still there!" And he opened his mouth in a big grin to demonstrate, making me laugh despite myself.

"You're right, I know, I'm being silly," I said. "But it felt so real, not like any other dream I've had before. I mean, I was having a completely different dream and he just – burst in there. It felt like it was really him, if you know what I mean."

"I don't," said Aristo firmly. "But I do think you didn't like that innkeeper, and your imagination is running riot. Now come on, let's get back to bed, and let all these people," he gestured towards Nicias and his own slaves, "get back to bed too."

"All right," I said with a sigh, getting up, but I still felt uncomfortable. "Are you sure I shouldn't go back and check on him?" I asked Aristo as he steered me towards the guest room.

"Yes," said Aristo firmly, "I am absolutely sure. Now good night." And with that he closed the door on Nicias and me, and I heard his footsteps padding away down the corridor to his own bedroom.

*****

It took me a little while to fall back asleep, but I did eventually. For a while, I must have slumbered without dreaming. But that peace did not last.

This time, I was unaware of any real surroundings. I was in darkness. Not a dark room, or a dark place, but simply darkness, all around, and the darkness was somehow holding me, as if it were a physical thing.

Footsteps started to come towards me. Two sets of footsteps, moving awkwardly, almost shuffling. One set of bare feet, and one set with one bare foot and one cheap summer sandal.

I turned around. Two figures were stumbling through the void, coming in my direction. The barefoot man walked behind the other. Even before I could make out their faces, I knew who they were.

Decimus was covered in blood. Blood was spattered across his face and up and down his legs, and his tunic and his one small sandal were covered in it. But mostly it poured from his throat – and it was still pouring, even as he moved, the blood just kept flowing and flowing down his side from a gaping wound in his neck – more blood than any one human body could possibly contain, and it wouldn't stop. His eye bulged even more around the black and purple bruise, even more teeth were missing and his hair was matted against his head, full of gore and sweat. Behind him, Xanthias' head lolled as he stumbled along, his neck one big blue and green bruise, his eyes and tongue sticking out of his head.

I waited for what felt like forever as they slowly grew closer and closer. Finally, Decimus stood right in front of me, so close I could smell the taverna's cheap wine on his breath.

"You didn't come," he rasped.

"I didn't come," I replied, tears welling up and flowing unchecked down my face.

"Why didn't you come?"

I had no answer for that.

"We waited," he went on, unbearably. "We held that door for so long. But we couldn't hold it forever, and you didn't come."

I sank to the floor of nothingness and bowed my head but Decimus would not let me escape his accusing eyes. His bloodied hand gripped my hair and forced my head up to look at him.

"Since you would not help me when I still lived," he growled, "you can at least bury my body, and help my soul to cross the river Styx." I nodded, his hand still in my hair, pulling it tight. "The innkeeper threw my body in a cart and covered it with dung to stop the smell. The driver will reach the gate of Megara this morning. If you ever loved me, catch that cart and give my body the rites it needs so that I may rest in peace." And with that, abruptly, he was gone and I was awake, sweat soaking through Aristo's best guest sheets.

I could not fail my friend again. A tiny part of me wondered if this really was just a dream – if I was racing off to Megara in the middle of the night for no reason like a fool. I hoped that was true. I hoped I would find nothing, and that I would meet Decimus and Xanthias that evening, lounging around the tavernas of Megara, enjoying their wine and their dancing girls.

But there was another part of me, the part that acts without thinking, the part that we share with the animals that run from an earthquake before it happens or the oracles that allow a god to enter their body and work through them. That part knew with absolute certainty that these were not dreams, and that I had lost one of my oldest and closest friends.

And so I ran. I ran as I have never run before (or since), I ran like Pheidippides, I ran like Atalanta. I left Nicias behind with orders to tell Aristo where I had gone and follow me in the morning. I didn't want him to slow me down. I ran and I ran and I ran, and I tried not to think, but just to keep my feet pounding on the rocky road all through the growing dawn.

I reached the city gates of Megara early in the morning, the sun high in the sky. Just outside the gates was another grimy-looking taverna, no better than the last one, but placed nearer the road. A cart stood by its walls, a ill-fed mule still tethered to it.

Breathing hard, harsh gasps of air, I started towards the cart, and immediately became aware that it was filled with dung. And underneath the dung, my desperate lungs could just about make out another smell as well – something metallic, and something almost meat-y. I closed my eyes for a moment. I wanted to cry, but no real tears would come. I walked slowly around the side of the cart.

It was the sandal I saw first. The toe of that one, cheap summer sandal was just poking out from the bottom of the pile of dung. There was a bit of hay stuck to it.

Before I could move, a small, dirty little man emerged from the taverna and went red in the face when he saw me. "Hey!" he shouted. "Get away from that cart!"

At the sound of his yelling, I noticed the guards on the city gate a little way off stand up a bit straighter and take notice.

"What's in it?" I asked loudly. Very loudly. I saw one of the guards start to move towards us.

"Nothing!" cried the driver, going white as a sheet. He glanced over his shoulder, saw the guard headed in our direction, and fled.

"Stop that man!" I shouted, and the guard took off after him. Heedless of the filth and the smell, I used my hands to pull the muck off the dead – very dead – body of my friend. Xanthias, even more pungent, lay beneath him. "I'm sorry," I whispered to both of them. "I'm so, so sorry. I could have saved you. I should have saved you. I'm sorry." I took another breath, holding up my hand to my mouth, which did no good as it was covered in dung. "I will save your souls," I said, "I promise. I will at least save your souls."

I looked up to see a small crowd gathered around me, including another innkeeper. Although this second taverna looked no more appealing than the first, he seemed to be genuinely horrified by what he saw.

"Tell the guards to arrest the owner of the taverna in the woods just off the main road," I said to my little group of witnesses. I looked down at the cart and now, finally, the real tears came, hot and wet. "And then, we have a funeral to arrange."

FINIS

THE HAUNTED HOUSE

Inspired by Pliny, *Letters*, 7.27.5-11

"Do you believe in ghosts?" asked Secundus.

Sura put down his wine-cup thoughtfully. It was still half full. He picked up a dried fig to chew on while he thought about it.

"I don't know," he said, after much deliberation. "Sometimes, I think I do. Other times, I think they are just the tricks of a fevered imagination." He set down his plate and picked up the cup again. "Do you believe in ghosts?" he asked.

"Well," said Secundus, putting down his own cup firmly and re-settling himself on his dining couch, "let me tell you a story."

"Oh gods," muttered Sura into his wine, but Secundus did not hear him.

"It's a Greek story," said Secundus, "so make of that what you will."

"The Greeks are very good at telling stories," said Sura.

"Obviously," agreed Secundus. "But I think you will find this one most intriguing. And it certainly inclines me to believe that there is more to the other world than fever dreams and the visions of those who are sick in the mind."

And this is the story he told.

*****

Among the woods and twisting paths that curl around the rock of the Acropolis, just below the dark places where the young go to do the things they want to do in the dark, are the homes of the wealthy; gleaming in washed stone and bright red tile, well-kept flowering vines trailing gracefully across their walls and porticos.

But among them stood a house that was quite different. It was big, a rich man's mansion to be sure, but the walls and the roof were crumbling. The vines had almost overtaken the house, their long fingers creeping in to the windows and the doorways. The crumbling mud-bricks showed signs of unrepaired wear around the edges, and holes where burglars had tried their luck, optimistically hoping there might be something of value inside. The stones of the foundations were full of lichen in every crack, and the some of the roof tiles had fallen in. The wood of the door was damp and flaked away in your fingers, and no light shone from anywhere in the house or its grounds. It was an aberration, a hole where a handsome home should have been, a gaping chasm draining the life from the elegant villas surrounding it.

The house was in a prime location; not far from where the Roman Agora is now, with a stunning view across the city towards the Lykavittos Hill. It was advertised for sale or rent – but for a price more suited to a stall at the flea market than a vast, empty house. A small stall, at that.

Athenodorus, the Stoic, had recently arrived in Athens and was looking for somewhere to rent. The owner had been hoping for a fool who would take it at the price and ask no questions, but Athenodorus was no fool; he went straight to the nearby fountain and asked the women there to tell him about the house. Several would only shake their heads and walk away, but a few of the younger ones we were willing to stay and talk to him.

"No one has stayed even one night there in years," said one, "but my husband told me a lot of people tried to rent it, about ten years ago or more."

"A lot of people?" asked Athenodorus. "You mean it was a big household, or two households living together?"

"No, I mean a lot of different people, one after the other!" she replied. "People would come, rent the house, move in, and then, within a month or two, they would die there. Then someone else would come and rent it, and the whole thing would start again, until no one was willing to so much as set foot in the place any more."

"They died?" said Athenodorus. "What did they die of?"

"No one knows," said the first girl, but then another took up the story.

"They wasted away," she said. "Every morning they would come out of the house with eyes bulging, barely able to move because they'd had no sleep. Night after night, it would get worse and worse, until they no longer had enough energy to eat or drink. And even in bright sunlight, they would look at things that weren't there and jump at noises no one else could hear, as if whatever they saw and heard at night was so terrible that it had imprinted itself on their eyes and ears so they still saw and heard it even when it wasn't there."

"It was fear," said the first woman. "They died of fear itself – constant, never-ending fear."

"In this world, there are many more things that frighten us than those that can really crush us, you know," said Athenodorus, "and we often suffer far more in our imaginations than in reality. But what was it? What had frightened them so much?"

"They wouldn't really talk about it," said the second woman. "But we live next door, and sometimes, in the darkest part of the night, we hear weird clanking noises, like iron clashing against something. Once, leaning out of the window on a hot summer night, I even heard what sounded like clanking chains." Both women shuddered and pulled their veils closer about their heads and shoulders.

"That house has been empty and abandoned for a long time now," said the first woman. "I suppose you'll be looking elsewhere for somewhere to rent?"

"Not at all," said Athenodorus, looking up at the wretched shell of the house. "I am curious about everything there is in this world, the bad as well as the good. I am excited to rent this house and find out what's been happening inside it!"

"You're not afraid of it at all?" exclaimed the first woman.

"The human mind is very good at creating evil where there is no evil," said Athenodorus. "It is too easy to hear something spoken of in a vague or confusing way and think the worst, to imagine that some personal grudge is far worse than it is, or to dream up terrible possible futures in which our enemies go to the worst possible lengths to utterly destroy us, instead of whatever small jab or petty vengeance they are more likely to actually do. But life is not worth living, and there is no limit to our sorrows, if we indulge our fears to the greatest possible extent. I will not be afraid of this house, or of whatever it is that walks its empty rooms. For it seems to me, it was their own fancies that destroyed the people who tried to rent it before, not anything that might or might not be in the house itself."

Both women hastily spread their hands forward from their hearts to ward off evil, shook their heads, and turned back toward their homes, the older murmuring, "Good luck!" as she walked past. But Athenodorus went straight to the manager to rent the house.

None of the manager's staff would come anywhere near the site, so Athenodorus had to have his own people set up everything he needed. Luckily, his needs were fairly few. Inside, the house was as neglected as it had appeared from the outside. It was a good thing that it was sheltered by the rock of the Acropolis, for it seemed like every nook and cranny had its own draft, and everywhere you went, there was a chill breeze blowing at you from somewhere. There was very little light, for the thick vines crawling all over the shell of the building blocked what sunlight there was, straining to peek in from the outside. The small courtyard, dwarfed by the looming presence of the house's over-sized rooms all around it, was so overgrown that you could barely put your feet on the ground. Most of the walls were bare, their surface pockmarked with rough terracotta, but here and there a faded fresco allowed the dark eyes of a nymph, the strong arms of a heroic youth, or the delicate wings of a bird to peek through towards the newcomers as they tramped through the property with their belongings. Nearly all the furniture and other household items belonging to previous occupants had been taken away or looted over the years, but in the corner of one of the bedrooms, Athenodorus found a cracked piece of a beautifully painted decorative pot. It showed the head and torso of Persephone, her arms outflung, her eyes wide, being dragged off to the underworld by Hades in his chariot.

As evening fell, Athenodorus had the slaves make up a bed for him in the *andrōn*, the men's drinking-room in the front part of the house. Its tiled floor would ensure that anything approaching him – whether human, animal, or something else – would be heard well in advance. He had them provide him with writing tablets, a stylus, and a lamp, so that he could spend the night working. He was determined that he would not be frightened by any spectre of his own fevered mind's imaginings, but would observe only what was real and true. So he sat upright with his back against the wall, the lamp shining brightly next to him, and focused all his attention on his writing. He was working on a treatise on the education of boys and young men that he had been trying to finish for some time. He dismissed the slaves to the innermost rooms of the house and they scurried out, checking over their shoulders every few seconds as another creak, groan, or nightly noise startled them. But eventually Athenodorus could hear nothing but the crickets chirruping outside, and his own breathing.

For a while, all was peaceful. But as the night deepened and drew toward its darkest hour, another sound penetrated the gloom and the shadows. Initially distant, it sounded like the clanging of a hammer on iron. Then, as it got louder, it became the sound of iron chains, clanking. At first it seemed to be coming from somewhere a little way off, perhaps around the edges of the grounds of the house. Athenodorus was positioned near the street, and in that direction all was quiet.

But, as he bent his head over his writing, concentrating fiercely, the sound started to come nearer and nearer. Now it was in the empty store room next to the *andrōn*. The sound of rattling chains hitting the floor crept across the room, coming closer and closer to the wall the two rooms shared. He could hear the clanging of iron scraping across the stone floor, moving along the wall.

Now it was out in the hallway, near the entrance to the house. And now those clanking, rattling chains were being dragged across the hall; now they clattered into the doorway; and now onto the tiled floor of the *andrōn* itself...

Finally, Athenodorus looked up from his writing. By the light of the lamp he could see, standing between him and the doorway to the hall, the image, almost the shadow, of an old man. The figure was emaciated and filthy, his clothes gone to rags, his skin mottled and caked with mud. He had a long, flowing beard that fell in knots and tangles all the way down to his waist, and his tousled hair stood on end, sticking out at all angles from the skin stretched thinly across his knobbly skull. On his hands and his feet were large iron fetters with iron chains attached. The man was staring straight at Athenodorus with bulging eyes, his mouth open but no sound coming out of it. The only sound was the continued clashing of the iron chains as he held out his hands and his feet towards the philosopher and shook his wrists as vigorously as his worn bones would allow.

Athenodorus looked the spectre straight in the eye and held its gaze. He remained seated on the bed, the apparition standing in the middle of the floor of the room. Slowly, the old man reached forward with one shackled hand and beckoned the philosopher to come to him.

Athenodorus held a hand up and said, "Wait a little." Then he bent his head over his writing once more, to continue with a particularly intricate paragraph on the importance of maintaining the interest of young boys in the classroom, to facilitate their learning. With his head bent close to his tablet and his eyes down, he could no longer see the old man, who cast no real shadow, but seemed almost to be made up of shadows himself. But he could still hear him, for the ghoul stood over him as he wrote, rattling the chains dangling from its wrists over his head.

Finally, the paragraph finished, Athenodorus looked up, and saw the spectre standing and beckoning to him once more. So he picked up the lamp, stood up, and gestured to the phantom to show him the way. The old man led him back through the house, the chains on his legs dragging across the floor and making the most horrendous scraping sound the whole way, but leaving no permanent mark on the stones. Athenodorus followed, grasping his stylus in one hand, just in case, but otherwise showing no outer sign of even the slightest level of concern. Their progress was slow, for the old man seemed to be weighed down by his chains, though when Athenodorus tried once to lean down and pick them up, they passed straight through his hand.

After some time spent inching slowly down the hallway, Athenodorus could see shafts of moonlight fighting their way down through the undergrowth to the courtyard. The old man turned into the open court, and abruptly vanished before the philosopher's eyes. Athenodorus looked all over the courtyard by both moonlight and lamplight, but could see nothing. He marked the spot where the figure had disappeared by scraping the stones of the courtyard with his stylus, and returned quickly to the *andrōn*. He remained awake for the rest of the night, working on his treatise on education by the flickering light of the lamp, but he saw and heard nothing else out of the ordinary. There were only the chirruping of the crickets, the slight woosh of the drafts in the house, and his own laboured breathing.

The following morning, there was a great commotion at the old house. At the crack of dawn, a slave was sent running to fetch the owner, the manager, and the local magistrates. As the day warmed to be bright, hot, and clear, the women of the neighbourhood gathered around the fountain to watch as first the manager, then the owner, then the magistrate all turned up to the house, going straight into the *andrōn*, where they could be seen speaking with Athenodorus.

As the sun climbed higher in the sky, more slaves were sent for, and they were told to bring picks and shovels. Several flowed into the house, only to emerge looking tired, stressed, and shaken a few hours later. Eager inquiries asking them what was going on were met with frightened silence.

Inside, the house was equally chaotic. The *andrōn* was filled with irritable men; the owner, who spent most of his time pretending the house no longer existed and was not enjoying this reminder that it had not fallen down quite yet; the manager, who was wondering if he should have simply removed the 'For Rent' notice all together, and the magistrate, who was convinced he had been dragged out on a wild goose chase and who was being placated with the best wine Athenodorus could get hold of at short notice. Athenodorus himself, despite having not slept at all the night before, remained the calm at the centre of the storm. Meanwhile, the youngest and strongest of his own slaves worked with a few borrowed lads from the magistrate, digging up the courtyard at the spot Athenodorus had marked, where the ghost had vanished.

Athenodorus' patience was rewarded. Bringing water to the slaves while they worked, he found them just uncovering a long piece of white bone buried beneath the stones and the soil of the court. Encouraging them to proceed carefully, he stayed and watched as slowly they dug around the bones, uncovering more and more as they went. After almost a full day's work, as the sun was once more making its way towards the horizon, they found they had unburied a whole human skeleton, with iron fetters and chains binding the hands and the feet. The chains were twisted around the bones, digging into and corroding them, pinning them down in their place.

Whoever they had once belonged to, and whoever had killed him and trapped his corpse with iron in this place, it had obviously been long, long ago, for there was nothing else left.

The owner, manager, and magistrate came, and were duly horrified by what they saw. A small public burial was hastily arranged for the next day. There was no laying-out – everyone felt that the poor man had lain there without proper burial for long enough as it was. Athenodorus attended the procession, and with him the women from the fountain, who chanted the appropriate dirges. Around them stood the slaves who had worked to uncover the bones, no longer afraid of the helpless victim, and in the absence of any known family, the house's owner and manager and their wives offered libations. The bones were buried with all the proper rites and prayers, and Athenodorus had a small vase placed to mark the site. He continued to rent the house for many months before the time came for him to move on. He had it renovated and cleaned out and spruced up in every way, so that light shone in through the windows, the drafts were stopped, and the vines cut back to flow as gracefully and decoratively as those of their neighbours. The ghost was never seen or heard from again.

*****

Secundus finished his tale with a dramatic flourish and a wave of his arm, but Sura was unimpressed.

"I have heard that story before," he said. "Or something very similar, anyway. But it happened in Lugdunum, off up in Gaul somewhere, not in Athens."

"What was Athenodorus doing up in Lugdunum?" asked Secundus.

"Well, it wasn't him either," said Sura. "It was some random man, I forget the name."

"They probably just heard the story of what happened to Athenodorus and forgot the details," said Secundus.

Sura made a non-committal noise. It was late and he was

too tired to argue. "It's certainly a good tale," he said, and an old story, by the sounds of things. I wonder how much longer people will keep telling it?"

"For a hundred years or more at least, I should think," said Secundus. "It is memorable, if nothing else! Perhaps it will be told for another thousand years, or even two thousand."

"Nah," said Sura. "I don't think it will last that long." He sighed and stretched out his back and shoulders, standing up with a groan. "All this talk of ghosts and ghouls has tired me out old friend! Good night." And he drained his cup and went to bed.

FINIS

UNDER THE KITCHEN FLOOR

Inspired by Plautus, *Mostellaria*, 446-531

"Here's the place," said Philematium, using the large door knocker for its intended purpose.

"Nice," said Scapha approvingly. "He's got quite a bit of cash, your fella, hasn't he?"

"His dad has," said Philematium. "My Philolaches has nothing of his own – he had to borrow the money to set me free, and for this party. But the old man's rich as Croesus. He's been away for over a year, doing business in Egypt."

"That explains the party," said Scapha. It was a big party, and already in full swing as the door slave let them in, even though it was barely lunchtime. The crowd seemed nice enough, but Scapha was a realist.

"I hope you haven't got your hopes up just because he bought your freedom," she said. "You know all he really wanted was to stop you seeing anyone else. As soon as his dad gets back, you're on your own."

But Philematium wasn't listening. "Hello!" she said brightly to a young man fetching himself a cup of wine. "I don't think we've met – are you a friend of Philolachus?"

"Err, sort of," said the young man. "My name's Maccius. Are you enjoying the party?"

"We just got here – but I am now," said Philematium with a grin. After all, it would not be a good idea to put all her eggs in one basket. What if Scapha was right?

Philolaches was watching them with narrowed eyes from across the room. "Who's that, talking to Philematium?" he asked Tranio, his personal slave.

"I don't know, master," came the reply. "Probably a friend of hers. Or an ex-customer. But master, you can hardly marry her, after all. Let her talk to whomever she wants."

Philolaches opened his mouth to object, but was interrupted before he had the chance.

"Philolaches!" called his friend Callidamates from across the room. "I saw your father's ship in the harbour! Has he sent it home without himself in it?"

Philolaches felt sweat start to drip down his forehead, and found himself panting hard, his heart palpitating in his chest.

"Ye gods!" he exclaimed, the colour draining from his face. "His ship! So where is he? Is he coming here?" His mind started racing. "When is he coming? We need to get these people out of here!"

Tranio moved quickly over to the window and glanced down the street. "Um, I hate to upset you but it's a bit late for that – he's next door, talking to Simo."

Philolaches jumped up in a state of panic, and was sick on the floor. Philematium rushed to his side to coo over him, and the door slave went to fetch water, but the rest of the party carried on regardless. Even Callidamates had disappeared into the kitchen.

"Help me, Tranio!" gasped out Philolaches, through his misery.

Shit, thought Tranio to himself, but out loud he said, "Of course, master – leave it to me!"

Fighting his way through the party, he dashed out into the garden, hopped over the wall, and nipped around the back to make it look like he was approaching from further up the street. He was just in time to catch the old man, Theopropides, as he moved away from his neighbour's house and towards his own.

"Master! Master! Stop!!!" screamed Tranio as he ran down

the street.

"What?" the old man looked up in confusion. "Tranio, what are you doing? What's the matter with you?"

"Come away, master! Come away from the house at once!" Tranio grabbed the old man roughly by the arm and pulled him away into the street. A distant crash was heard from inside the house.

"Hey, that noise came from – Tranio what are you doing? Have you gone mad?" demanded Theopropides. He tried to resist and get back to his front door, but Tranio was much younger and stronger them him, and he was helpless as he was almost dragged away down the street.

"You must not touch the house, master! Not with one finger! It's – it's – " suddenly inspiration struck Tranio – "it's cursed!"

"Cursed? Someone cursed my house?" cried Theopropides.

"It's always been cursed! I mean, since you bought it!" insisted Tranio, pulling the old man as far away from the house and the noisy party as possible.

"Nonsense man! How could my house be cursed and I not even know it?" objected Theopropides.

"Well, I'll tell you!" said Tranio.

Theopropides stood and waited expectantly.

"I'll tell you in the taverna on the next street!" said Tranio. "You're going to need a stiff drink!"

*****

Tranio spent as much time as he could fussing over getting the old man the best seat in the taverna, going through the wine list as thoroughly as possible, letting the barman serve everyone else in the bar first, and sending back the first cups of wine because he insisted they were the dregs and not good enough for his master, but eventually he had no choice. He had run out of distractions and would have to come up with something to say about why Theopropides' house was cursed.

"Well you see, master, it's like this."
"Yes?"
"Well, you see, it's like this."
"Yes?"
"It's like this you see – "
"Get on with it, man!"

And so Tranio concocted a story.

"We'd noticed strange omens about the house. Eerie sounds were heard in the night, there were strange knockings at all sorts of times of day. Sometimes it even seemed as if we could hear the sounds of a raucous party going on, when really there was nobody there and nothing was happening. Then one morning, your son – Philololachus, your son – he went in to the dining room for breakfast and found a message scrawled across the wall in blood – *terribilis est locus iste*! This place is terrible! That was when we realised that the house was cursed – it has been polluted by a terrible crime that was committed within its walls!"

"Wait a minute," said Theopropides. "We've lived in this neighbourhood for years. How could a crime as terrible as you suggest have been committed in the house and we've never heard of it?"

"It was committed a long time ago," said Tranio, "now, do you want to hear the story or not?" Theopropides nodded his head to indicate that he did, and Tranio continued.

"So, the message had given us a clue. Obviously the house is terrible because some terrible crime has been committed there. But we didn't know what and we didn't know how to go about finding out. The knocking went on and on, all day and all night, and the moaning sounds were getting worse, but we were scratching our heads, not knowing where to start. Then one morning another message appeared, even bigger letters, all in blood – *DICO*. 'I say!' But what did it say? We couldn't work it out at all. Then the next morning another message – *DICIMO*. Well, that didn't make any sense at all, and we wondered if maybe whoever cursed the house was a poor man who couldn't spell very well. But then the next day it changed again – it said *MUIDICIMOH*. Which is, of course, *HOMICIDIUM* backwards – 'murder!' The house was polluted because someone had been murdered there! And we might even have met and talked to the murderer – it was probably the very man who sold you the house!"

"Wait – you mean our neighbour Polydorus, who moved a little way up the street? You think he murdered someone?!"

"Polydorus is one to watch, you know. He keeps many secrets. Anyway, on with the story. Once we knew a murder had been committed on the premises, we knew we had to do something about it. So we started a thorough search of the whole house, looking for evidence. We realised that if the murder had been covered up, that meant the body was probably still in the house, buried somewhere on the grounds without a proper funeral or anything! And when we looked, we even noticed that the floor in the kitchen looks a lot newer than the rest of the floors..."

"Ye gods!" cried Theopropides, rising. "We must exhume the body at once, and lay it to rest with proper burial rites! Call the undertaker! Search the house – especially the kitchen!"

"No, no!" cried Tranio in a panic. "We don't know for sure it's in the kitchen! We have no idea where the body is! But we know that there *is* a body, and there was a murder, because, um, you see – his ghost told us! The victim's ghost!"

"What?" Theopropides sat down with a thud, shocked.

"Yes!" said Tranio. "If you just let me get on with my story, I'll explain. It was late at night. Your son – Philolaches, your son – he had been out, dining with friends – well educated, cultured friends – rich friends – good types of friends to have. Anyway, he came back late and we all went to bed, but I – silly me! – I'd left a lamp burning in the dining room. I just plum forgot about it! Anyway, so we all went to bed. And then, in the middle of the night I heard a terrible scream coming from your son's bedroom!"

"From my son's bedroom?" said Theopropides. "I thought you said the lighted lamp was in the dining room?"

"Well yes, so it was, but – well that didn't have anything to do with it really, it was just something else that happened that night," said Tranio, with only the slightest edge of desperation creeping into his voice. "Let me continue. Philolaches came running out of his bedroom, screaming. He was in a terrible state, eyes wide with shock, trembling all over, every hair standing on end. 'I saw him!' he cried. 'He came to me! He came to me in my sleep!'"

"Hang on, hang on, just a minute," said Theopropides, putting down his wine cup firmly and looking Tranio right in the eyes. "Are you telling me this was all a dream?"

"Yes, the ghost came to him in a dream," said Tranio, "and he said – "

"In a dream?" repeated Theopropides, motioning to the barman to bring the bill. His previous alarm had completely subsided and he was now giving Tranio a suspicious look.

"Well of course in a dream, the man's been dead sixty years, how else do you expect him to talk to anyone?" cried Tranio. "Now are you going to let me tell this story, or not?"

Theopropides sighed and motioned to the slave to continue. Tranio drew breath to speak but before he could say a word, something else suddenly occurred to the old man.

"Sixty years?" he said. "I thought you said you suspected Polydorus? He's barely fifty!"

"I told you, he has many secrets," said Tranio. "He's obviously been lying about his age. Anyway, where was I? Oh yes. 'I saw him!' Philolaches cried, tearing at his nightclothes in his terror and discomfort. 'I saw him! He came at me, and he was terrible to behold! He was an old man, his face haggard, his eyes popping out from their sockets! His fingers were charred from the funeral pyre…'"

"I thought you said there wasn't a proper funeral?"

Tranio ignored this entirely and carried on.

"His fingers were charred from the funeral pyre, and he was weighed down by heavy iron chains which dangled from his wrists and feet. Philolaches could hear the chains clanking as he dragged them across the ground. Clank! Clank! Clank!

The spectre reached out to him with his shrivelled hands, the chains flying up into his face, and he cried, 'Help me, Philolachus! Help me!' Your son was terrified, but he thought of you and how brave you would be if it were happening to you, and he drew himself up to his full height, and he looked the ghost square in its terrible, hollow eyes with the skin all pulled back around the skull, and he said, 'Who are you, and how can I help you?' 'I was a guest of the man who owned this place, Polydorus,' said the ghost. 'I was a traveller from across the sea, an old family friend – I was married to his wife's cousin's barber's patron. My name is Diapontius!'"

"His name literally meant "across the sea?" said Theopropides.

"It was his work name," said Tranio desperately, and he ploughed on.

"'I was a rich merchant, and when Polydorus saw how much gold I carried with me, he murdered me, buried my body without any funeral rites at all, and stole my gold! And so now I am doomed to haunt this place, forever denied passage across the Styx and entry into the underworld, and you must leave this house forever, for it is cursed!'"

"Well, that settles it!" cried Theopropides. "We must search the house morning, noon, and night, until we find the body so we can bury it properly and lay this ghost to rest!"

"Alas! That won't help!" cried Tranio. "You see, the ghost explained; 'I am doomed, doomed to haunt this house for one hundred and twenty-five years, no matter what you do!' 'That's terrible!' said Philolaches. 'Why?' 'I'll tell you why,' said the ghost. 'Because,' said the ghost," (Tranio drummed his fingers on the table, desperately stalling for time and wracking his brains for a sensible reason), "'because,' he said... ' because Hades will not let me descend to the underworld, because I died before my time. I must wait out my lifespan in this place, and only when my allotted time is reached will I be allowed to cross the river and join the eternal dead in their kingdom!'"

"One hundred and twenty-five years?" sputtered

Theopropides. "No man has ever lived so long!"

"He was a very healthy man," said Tranio irritably, "had his life not been tragically cut short. So you see, we cannot possibly return to the house! You should go back to Egypt straight away, and stay there safely until we can buy a new home on your behalf."

"Perhaps you're right," said Theopropides slowly. "I certainly do not want to live in a cursed and haunted house!" He quickly made a sign against evil, and took a small amulet out from underneath his tunic, kissed it, and put it back again. "But I have treasures of my own in there, Tranio. I must go back for them."

"Let me, master! I'll fetch whatever you want for you!"

"No, no! These are my most precious treasures, and their location is known only to myself. I mean to keep it that way. No, I must brave this place to fetch them. Come Tranio! We are returning home!"

*****

As Tranio followed the old man out of the taverna and back towards the house, he was reasonably optimistic. He had kept Theopropides talking for a long time. Surely Philolachus would have ended the party and cleared out the guests by now?

But his hopes were dashed as they came up the street towards the house, for he could still hear singing, talking, and the occasional crash coming from inside.

"Master! Do you hear that? It's the ghost!" he cried, jumping in front of Theopropides and standing between the old man and the house.

"Ye gods!" said Theopropides. "How am I to get in?"

"I shall go ahead of you, master, and clear away the spirit so you can get in – but be careful! Touch nothing but your treasures! Don't look around you and don't so much as brush the doorframe! In fact – close your eyes, take my hand, and I'll lead you through the house!"

Theopropides appeared to think for a minute. "Very well," he said. "I'll close my eyes, until we reach the bedroom. Then *you* must close *your* eyes while I fetch my things."

"Good plan, master!" said Tranio. Taking the old man's hand while Theopropides used the other to cover his eyes, Tranio led him carefully through the front door and into the house. A party guest moaned and vomited into a plant pot as they went past.

"What was that?" said Theopropides.

"Can you hear the spirit moaning, master?!" said Tranio, hurrying on. As they went past the *impluvium* pool, another party guest, laughing, toppled backwards and fell in with a loud splash.

"What was that?" said Theopropides.

"The ghost's chains are dragging across the floor and through the *impluvium*, master! Can you feel the splash?" Tranio pulled the old man away before a second guest followed their friend in. As they headed towards the bedrooms, both suddenly stumbled over the prone form of another party guest, lying on the floor.

"Argh! What was that?" said Theopropides.

"I think the ghost is trying to show us where he's buried, master! He's lying prone on the floor!" cried Tranio, kicking the whimpering man quietly behind him.

They had almost reached the bedroom door when a voice from behind them cried, "Father! I can explain everything!"

Tranio dropped the old man's hand and made desperate waving motions at Philolaches, trying to get him to stop talking. But it was too late. Theopropides took his hand from his eyes at the sound of his son's voice and looked up. He turned himself in a slow circle, taking in the chaos around him.

"Philolaches?" he said, in amazement at first, which quickly turned to anger. "What exactly is going on here?"

"Father – hello – I can explain everything, honestly, I – "

"Why are you having a party in a haunted house?"

There was an uncomfortable silence.

"Err, pardon me?" said Philolaches.

Light seemed to dawn on Theopropides. "There is no ghost, is there?" he said, turning to Tranio coldly.

"Um, master, I..." Tranio gave up and fled across the hall to the family *lararium*, where they kept a small altar dedicated to the household gods. He leapt on top of it, saying, "May the gods protect me!"

"Is *this* where the money I sent for investments has gone?" thundered Theopropides, as the drunken party guests started to realise what was happening and quickly and quietly make their exits. Philematium started to move towards Philolaches, but he looked at her with panic and anger, and she quietly slipped away.

"Oh Father, we've spent very little money, really," said Philolaches, as a party guest knocked over a priceless decorative vase in their hurry to leave, and the chef slipped by with a tray of rare delicacies to store in the kitchen.

"Young man, when I am through with you and that impudent slave..." started Theopropides, but he was interrupted again, this time by Callidamates, who was approaching, looking reasonably upright, with his arm around Scapha.

"Let me interrupt, good sir," he said, putting a firm hand on Theopropides' shoulder. "I am, as you know, financially independent and very rich," there was a definite smirk playing around his mouth as he said this, "and I have reason to be grateful to your son for throwing this little gathering, or shindig," and here he squeezed Scapha's shoulders while she looked up at him adoringly. "So to save my friend – and his loyal man here," pointing at Tranio, "from unnecessary hardship and/or beating, I will offer to pay the full costs of this party, and all the damages."

"Just *this* party, or all of the parties since the master went away?" said Tranio, but he said it quietly, and to himself, and perhaps the household gods.

Theopropides thought about this. "All the costs?" he said slowly. "And the damages? Including replacing that vase?"

He'd never liked it much and was quite enjoying the thought of getting a better one.

"Indeed, sir," said Callidamates grandly. "Your son has given me a priceless gift in this young woman." At that, he and Scapha kissed noisily, and everyone else looked away for a moment, as there are few things in this world less sexy to watch than very drunk people kissing.

"Very well," said Theopropides. "You can come down from the altar, Tranio. Callidamates has saved you a lashing. But Philolaches, I expect you to help clear up. And if this ever happens again, I can assure you, you will not find me so generous."

And with that, the excitement was over. The guests returned home, and things started to settle back down into the old, quiet patterns of life, from before Theopropides went away.

Maccius watched sadly from the atrium as the last of the guests left. 'That's a shame,' he thought to himself, "I was rather enjoying those parties.' Since there was nothing else to see, he drifted back to lie where his body had been hastily and improperly buried under the kitchen floor, and while away the years twiddling his ethereal thumbs in boredom.

FINIS

THE DEAD MARRIAGE

Inspired by Apuleius, *Metamorphoses*, 9.29-31

On the edge of town, so close to the graves that she could smell them, a woman hesitated outside a small hovel. She reached into her cloak and removed a tiny, hidden necklace in the shape of a letter T, which she kissed and put away in a coin purse. Nervously patting her elaborately styled hair, she knocked, waited for an answering call, and ducked inside.

The hovel's only occupant sat at a tall table, writing labels on a series of dull, dirty jars. Her dark hair was wild and unkempt, and as her visitor peered in horror through the shadows, she saw a flash of snakeskin ripple through the greying curls. The woman's funereal black dress matched the grime and smoke stains that covered her tiny home. A basket at her feet held a collection of crude dolls made of wood, wax and lead; another by the table contained a pile of papyrus scrolls.

"Well, this is a surprise," said the black-clad woman. Unlike her appearance, her voice was surprisingly normal, not at all the withered-old-crone-croak her customers often expected. "I know you – the miller's wife. The atheist. You don't believe in the gods."

"I believe in One God," her visitor mumbled awkwardly. "But that's not why I'm here."

"Obviously." The witch sat back in her chair and patted

her lap for her black cat to leap up to her, but the cat was having none of it, and stayed put in his bed.

"I've heard that you can enchant men's minds," continued the nervous monotheist. "Make them believe what you want them to. Make them think differently."

"Sometimes," came the reply. "Usually women come to me because they want men to fall in love with them, or because they want a man to fall out of love with them and leave them alone. Which is it to be today?"

"I want my husband to forgive me," said the visitor.

"Ah." The witch paused and sucked in her teeth. "That's trickier."

There was a silence, until the woman realised she was supposed to be filling it.

"He caught me in bed with my lover," she said. "The boy's just a kid really, even younger than me, though not by much. His beard is mostly fluff. My husband announced that since we share everything, we should share the young man too, and took him away for the rest of the night. Then in the morning he had him whipped, and threw me out into the street with a note of divorce."

"I see," said the witch, poking around in her pile of scrolls. "So you want your husband to love you again?"

"I want him to forgive me," said the woman. "I want him to take me back. I want him to be blind to my lovers, like he was before."

"Pffffft," said the witch, heaving her breath out of her mouth. "I can try, but no promises." She pulled out one of the wax dolls and held it up for inspection. "Love is easy, you see," she said, holding it out towards the visitor. "When most people say 'love,' what they really mean is sex. A bit of heat here," – she gestured to the doll's private parts, – "and a little heat here and here," – gesturing to its heart and head – "and that's all anyone really wants. Besides, the lover is generally fairly besotted themselves, and that helps. But you're not in love yourself. You don't really want *him*, you just want to live in his house. And you don't want love or lust, you want forgiveness, which is much harder."

The woman turned away for a moment, biting her lip. Then she seemed to come to some decision.

"If you can't make him forgive me," she said, "if you can't make him take me back – I want him gone."

"You want him to leave town?" There was a glint in the witch's eye. She knew that wasn't her visitor's meaning, but she was going to make her say it.

"I want him dead," the woman replied.

"Now that," said the witch with a smile, "I can do."

*****

In the heat of the day, slaves and animals trudged weary circles together, grinding flour at the mill. A small group of overseers strolled the grounds free of tethers, wielding whips and canes. The canes were for the mules and donkeys which, blind-folded, were spurred on to go round and round and round, eternally pulling the millstone like an endless spinning top. The whips were for the human slaves who worked alongside the animals. Branded on their foreheads to make sure they could not run away, clothed in a skimpy bit of loincloth per man, most of the slaves were shackled to their posts, their backs criss-crossed with welts from the lash. A layer of fine white flour had settled onto the sweat on their skin, giving them an eerie and other-worldly appearance. They did not speak; they barely breathed. A moment's hesitation and the lash came down again, even more easily than the cane was put to the animals. The animals were worth more.

Lucius was luckier. As a house slave, he was bathed and clothed and well fed. He hated going near the mill, hated seeing what his life could have been – could still be at the whim of his master. He could not meet the eyes of the donkeys, never mind the men in there.

But today, he had no choice. He scurried across the grounds of the mill with a note for the master, who was inspecting his goods – human, animal, and product. Lucius was especially nervous because he knew that the message was yet another plea for mercy from the mistress, who had gone to stay with her sister for a few days after their latest fight. He shuddered as he passed close to an overseer in the act of raising his whip to strike one of the mill-slaves. Lucius had to stop and take a deep breath to calm himself down before approaching the master, who sat a few feet away at a high table, going over his accounts. As Lucius approached the table, the note held out, a stir and the unusual sound of the slaves' voices raised to a low murmur made both of them look up towards the gate.

A woman had walked into the mill. Not the mistress, or any of her slaves. This was a woman no one there had ever seen before. And nor did they want to again, for she was clearly experiencing intense distress. She was in an appallingly dishevelled state, like a defendant in court who wants to arouse the sympathy of the jury by making themselves look as tired, stressed and pathetic as possible, except that she seemed to have gone too far for even the most easily moved jury to be able to stand to look at her. She was barefoot and half-clothed in rags. Her skin, which was more unnaturally white than the slaves' flour-coated bodies, showed through what was left of her dress. She looked starving, and her head hung down, her loose hair hanging in tangled clumps across her face. What could be seen of her expression was unutterably, unbearably sad. She had poured ashes over her head, and a grey trail of muck and soot tumbled down from her matted hair like blood.

She started to walk towards the miller at his desk. Her movements were stilted and awkward, her body hunched over and her feet dragging as if every step caused her pain. Lucius shrank back in revulsion while every other man in the grounds was gaping at her in horror, but the miller's reaction was quite different. His master seemed transfixed, gazing at the woman as if she were the most beautiful creature he had ever seen. A small smile played about his lips as he let his stylus fall and slowly stood up to greet her. His eyes were soft, softer than

Lucius had ever seen them – and certainly softer than they had ever been when he looked at his wife. He seemed oblivious to the shock of his slaves and the quiet muttering that was silenced only by the crack of the whip; he had eyes only for this woman.

Finally, the woman finished making her slow, limping way over to the miller. Her head was hanging, but she seemed to try to turn it coquettishly, her strangled hair falling back to reveal one bloodshot eye. The miller's smile widened and he looked at her hungrily. She leaned over and whispered something in his ear, laying a single hand on his arm. He smiled some more. Gently, she drew her hand down his arm to lace her brittle fingers in his and lead him across the yard to his private room.

After a moment or two of silence, the overseers cracked their whips once more and the endless grinding work of the mill began again. Lucius, his message undelivered, paused a moment before scurrying away, out of the range of the lash.

Several times that afternoon Lucius tried to return to deliver the mistress' message to his master, but every time he was told the same thing. The master had not yet emerged from his private room, and nor had the mysterious woman. As evening fell and the heat of the summer day finally shifted to the close warmth of evening, Lucius was at a loss what to do. He returned once more, to find the yard half-deserted. The chained slaves and animals were still there, but they sat on the ground, most of them laying their heads back and resting their eyes. Lucius followed the sounds of men arguing and something banging to the master's room, where he found the overseers huddled around the doorway. They had been calling the master for some time, it seemed, and there had been no answer. They had knocked, and were still knocking, but there was no response, and no sound from within.

"We should break the door down!" cried one.

"Are you mad?" demanded another. "Damage the master's property? Not to mention disturbing him while he's alone with a young woman! We'll all be crucified!"

"You didn't see the woman, mate," another told him. "If it was a woman. I think it was a demon sent from Hades. No woman should look like that."

"My sister looked like that when they buried her," muttered another.

"Gods damn the woman!" spat the first man. "To Hades with her! We need the master. There's no more grain to grind. And if you think he'll be happy about us just stopping work and downing tools, you've got another think coming! He'll crucify us for *that*, sure as you like."

A lot of general murmuring suggested that the first overseer had a point.

"Fine," agreed the second overseer eventually, "but don't break the door down. Don't damage his property any more than you have to. Break the hinges if you must, but leave the door intact."

Lucius leant forward to help two of the overseers pry the door hinges apart and lift the door itself free of them. That meant he got a full, clear view of what lay on the other side.

The miller hung from a beam in the roof, dead. He had obviously been dead for hours, and a slight smell had started to rise from his body in the summer evening warmth. The strange woman was nowhere to be seen.

Immediately, the overseers began to wail and beat their chests in a show of grief. Perhaps their grief was real – they had a cushy position in the mill, after all, and might not be so lucky with a new master. Lucius backed away and brought the news to the shackled slaves sitting in the flour dust outside. They simply looked at him once, and closed their eyes again. Not one of them dared to allow themselves a glimmer of hope that their next master might be better.

The sticky heat of the summer evening closing in, the overseers ordered the chained slaves to dig a grave quickly and buried the miller with little ceremony. Lucius went to bed, the mistress's letter still in his pouch.

*****

The next morning, the household's attempt to sleep late in the refreshing absence of both master and mistress was disturbed by the sound of a woman's wail approaching from the street. The slaves gathered nervously in the yard, the overseers clutching their whips and their canes. But, to everyone's relief, there was no sign of the mysterious woman from the day before. The wailing sound was coming from the miller's daughter, who had run there all the way from the next town over the hill, where she lived with her husband. No one wanted to have to tell her what had happened to her father, but it soon became clear that no one had to. She already knew.

The young woman had loosed her hair for mourning and was beating her breasts and keening a funeral dirge. The overseer pointed her silently towards the makeshift grave they had thrown together for her father and she sank to the freshly dug earth, her simple but pretty dress dragging in the dirt. For a little while, she just sat there and continued to offer her wailing and her self-flagellation in grief at her father's passing.

But she was stirred to action when a familiar face appeared among the growing crowd outside the mill. The miller's wife had come for the reply to her message, still buried in Lucius' pouch. When she realised what was happening, she tried to pull away, but too late – her stepdaughter had seen her.

"Wicked harpy!" screamed the young woman, throwing herself at her one-time childhood friend, attacking her with teeth and nails. "Harlot! Whore! Spawn of Clytemnestra! You have killed my father!" And she broke down weeping.

"Dear one, what are you talking about?!" exclaimed the wife, appearing to be genuinely shocked and confused.

"I saw him!" cried the daughter through her tears. "I saw him! Late last night, in the dark, in my bedroom, he came to me. I saw his face, pale, his eyes bulging and his throat bruised from the noose that was still around his neck! He could not have spoken with any human voice, but from the depth of his soul he told me everything."

"Who? Who came to you?" Lucius could hear the crowd repeating the question all around the street.

"My father! He said he divorced you for adultery but you would not accept it! You went to that witch on the edge of town," here she scanned the crowd, but the black-clad woman was not among them, "and you ordered his death! The witch sent a spirit to fetch him and drag him down to the underworld!" At this, the daughter threw her whole body at her stepmother and beat the other woman to the ground, pummelling her with her fists and scratching at her eyes. All the while, the stepmother screeched her desperate denials, but she was not convincing anyone. Her step-daughter's raw emotion was much more moving.

Finally, the mill's slaves pulled their master's daughter away and held her back. Shakily, bruised and bleeding, the miller's wife – or rather, his widow – got to her feet.

"I'll come back inside now," she said quietly. "We need to carry out the proper mourning rituals, and then divide the estate."

The daughter laughed, a hard, cold laugh. "There's no point in pretending, bitch! My father divorced you. I know it. He told me. And even if he hadn't, you were married without *manus*. That means you are still the responsibility of your own father, not your husband, and you are not entitled to anything of his. This house, this mill, and everything in it," she glanced around at the slaves and the animals, "is mine. Get out. I never want to see you again."

The miller's wife looked for help among the crowd, but found none. Hesitantly, she drew out her little T-shaped necklace and held it forward to some particular bystanders she seemed to recognise, displaying it like a token, but they turned their faces away and pretended not to know her. Finally, she limped away, her walk no less stilted and uncertain than the apparition that had appeared to her husband the day before.

For nine days, the traditional mourning rites were observed. On the tenth day, the daughter took control of her inheritance. She wanted nothing more to do with the place that had seen her father die in such a strange way. Every slave and every pack animal in the mill was sold.

FINIS

A WARNING

Re-told from Propertius, *Elegies*, 4.7 and 4.8

There are Shades, of a sort; death does not end it all.

Cynthia had only recently been buried by the roadside, a quick, cheap funeral headed up by the slaves she had freed in her will. But I seemed to see her leaning over me as I tossed and turned in my empty bed, unable to sleep. Her eyes, those eyes that first grabbed me and trapped me, those bright blue eyes, such fine eyes – they were the same. Her hair was tumbled up as it was when she died; as it was when we buried her, all tousled golden curls pinned on top of her head.

But those once perfect golden curls were singed and burned around the edges, the marks of the funeral pyre clear to see. Her dress was half-burned, sitting charred against her side where the flames had consumed it. The blue beryl ring she always wore, that big ring whose marks could still be seen on my face, had been eaten by the fire. The stone had fallen out as the bronze setting had melted into her hand. Her fingers were brittle, and stripped down to the bone. Her lips, lips that I had kissed a thousand times and a thousand more, had been worn away by the waters of the river Styx.

But despite the ruin of her body, I could see from her expression that her mind was clear. She had not forgotten me, that was for sure.

"Sleeping soundly are you, my love?" she said, her voice dripping with sarcasm and contempt. "Have you forgotten me already?" She reached out a bony finger to stroke my cheek gently. "Have you forgotten all those nights I let down a rope to you from my window, and you snuck into my room, glancing about left and right to make sure no one had seen you wandering around the common streets of the Subura? Or the nights we threw caution to the wind, and made love at the crossroads, bodies heaving under our cloaks? Have you found a replacement for me already, so soon?"

"How could I forget you?" Her touch was gentle and sexy and brittle and creepy all at the same time. I shuddered, choking on rising bile at the thought of her dead hands on me. At the same time, I wept to see her like this. "You were my Muse," I told her, leaning back to move my face away. "You were all I thought about, night and day. Every poem, every line of verse, is about you. How could I ever forget you?"

"Pfft!" she snorted. "All those poems about how temperamental, cruel, and unfaithful I was, you mean? I think you *should* forget about those. And I hardly think it's true that you thought always of me and no other. I know for certain that you have spent quite a lot of time thinking about Phyllis as well, and Teia, and Flavia and Julia, too." She shook her head at me, and flecks of ash fell on my hair. "But if you remember me so well and I meant so much to you," she said, "how do you explain that sham of a funeral you barely honoured me with?"

I was silent, my mind for once empty of words. I waited to see if she would move away, but she was relentless.

"You abandoned me as I was dying!" she accused me, pointing that sharp bony finger at me, and I was silent, because I knew it was true. "You weren't there to call out my name! You couldn't give me those last few moments on this Earth, which were only my due after all the hours I gave you over the years. At my funeral, there wasn't so much as a watchman to shake a split cane to frighten away the evil spirits, never mind a proper rattle, and as my body was jostled about on the way to a hastily lit pyre, a broken tile cut my face." She turned her head to show me a deep gash down one side. There was very little blood, just a gaping hole in the skin of her cheek, where the lower part of the loose skin flapped down over her face.

"Just because you want a simple, poor man's funeral, which for some reason you delighted in telling me while we were in bed together, doesn't mean that's what I wanted! And where were you, anyway? Were you at my graveside in your black funeral robe, weeping for me? No! If you were so embarrassed to be seen at a cheap funeral, outside the city gates, you could have ordered the undertakers to walk more slowly, and followed along at a distance. You could have paid someone to put nard on my pyre, or at least scatter it with cheap hyacinths! Did I mean nothing to you, in the end?"

I tried to respond, but the words stuck in my throat. I could deny none of it. I had stayed as far away from her funeral as I could. I had paid off the undertakers to dispose of her body quickly and efficiently, left the former and current slaves of her household to walk with it and honour the spirits at her tomb, and I had left. I didn't know what to say. But Cynthia was not yet finished.

"And as if all this wasn't bad enough," she declared, really warming to her theme, "as if all this wasn't insult enough to disturb my spirit and allow me no rest, on top of everything, you have my murderer still among your household!"

I was stunned. Murderer?

*****

It was two weeks earlier. Cynthia had gone to Lanuvium, supposedly to take part in the fertility rites of Juno Sospita. Hah! Fertility rites! As if she wasn't in the habit of visiting the old woman several times a year to make sure she wouldn't be fertile. She had gone there with some other man, some idiot with more money than sense. I heard them leave, Cynthia driving the cart like a madwoman, hanging over the end of the shaft with the reins loosely gripped in her hands, shouting and laughing.

Well, I thought, fine, then. She has gone off with her new tagalong – I will find ways to entertain myself. And so I had my slave, Lygdamus, bring Phyllis and Teia over to my house, two rather lovely girls whose profession you would never guess to look at them – they have no sores or scars, just the tiniest, most discreet brand sitting under their dresses. It was a beautiful, warm evening, and peaceful, with only the sound of the chirping ciccadas and the distant murmur of the night time traffic from the city streets to disturb us. We set up three couches in the courtyard garden and settled down together. Lygdamus acted as cup-bearer, keeping our wine cups well topped up and mixed with only a small amount of water. Magnus the dwarf came to play the boxwood flute for us and Phyllis danced with castanets. Teia devoted her attention entirely to me.

Suddenly, we heard a commotion from the front of the house. We heard the front door slammed shut, and the sound of shouting voices.

Before we could move from our seats, Cynthia burst into the courtyard in a fury, the door slave hovering nervously and ineptly behind her. Her hair hung loose about her shoulders and her face was contorted with rage as she swept towards the couches, screaming bloody murder at anyone who dared to get in her way. Nomas, her body-woman, trailed in behind her, looking ashamed and embarrassed at this ridiculously over-the-top display.

Cynthia flung herself first at Phyllis, then at Teia, tearing at their soft faces with her fingernails. The neighbours on both sides woke up and leaned out of their windows and over the walls, yelling at us to be quiet, only adding to the general cacophony. Phyllis and Teia fled, their hair flying behind them, clutching their thin dresses to their chests, and took refuge in the taverna down the street, where their several regular customers would give them a warmer welcome.

Cynthia slapped me hard across the face, that big ring of

hers catching my cheek and leaving a big purple bruise that is still there now. Then she turned her attention to Lygdamus, rooting him out from under the couch, where he was hiding.

"You!" she shouted. "You organised this, you worthless, ungrateful – "

"Please, Master!" cried Lygdamus, raising his head to stare wide-eyed at me, even as Cynthia gripped his hair with her left hand, pulling his head back and stretching his neck, giving her plenty of room to strike him with her right. "Please, tell her – it's not my fault!"

Drunk, sleepy, and confused, I raised my hands to the heavens as if to say, what can I do? I was as powerless in front of this onslaught as he was.

"He's mine!" screamed Cynthia, right in Lygdamus' face. "He's *mine*, and no other woman shall have him!"

"I'm yours, I swear Cynthia, I'm yours," I protested, throwing myself to the ground and grabbing her feet in supplication, washing them with my tears. Cynthia finally let go of Lygdamus, who scampered away to the atrium, where Nomas offered him a cup of my wine and a comforting arm.

"How will you prove it to me?" she demanded.

"I'll wash myself clean of any trace of another woman, I'll wash out all the sheets, I'll stay in the house and only go out for essentials, I'll spend all my time just waiting for you!" I wailed in desperation.

Cynthia drew herself up straight, apparently mollified. "*He*," she said, pointing furiously at Lgydamus, "he must be sold. Let him drag heavy chains by his ankles through the silver lodes in the mines. I do not want to see him here again."

I nodded mutely and dismissed the miserable-looking Lygdamus with a wave of my hand. He, shaking, was led away by Nomas to some back part of the house, and I heard her calling for Chef to make him a hot drink. My attention was completely focused on Cynthia, who led me to our bed, ripped off the sheets that had been polluted by the presence of another woman, and pulled me right down onto the bare couch to make up our quarrel in the usual way.

Afterwards, as we both raised ourselves up on our elbows to drink some fresh wine and recover our clothes, she bent down and gripped my face firmly in both her hands. She stared right into my eyes and repeated once more,

"You're *mine*."

*****

"You're *mine*," she said again, as once more her hands gripped my face – only this time, the fingers were worn down to the bone and her eyes stared out of a sunken face, her charred hair hanging down across her exposed cheekbone.

"What happened?" I whispered, afraid of the answer.

"The wine was pale, too pale," she said. "Break open Nomas' pots and you'll find the traces of her poisons in the potsherds. But it wasn't her idea, I'm sure of it. She is witless, and incapable of coming up with such a plan on her own. Lygdamus is the true culprit, he was the one who put her up to it. Prepare a white-hot iron for him and you'll soon get the truth out of him!"

"What do you want me to do?" I asked.

"First, brand and sell Lygdamus! And buy my slaves from Nomas. Like a fool, I freed her in my will – how could I know she'd bring my death about?! – and she is abusing all of my loyal slaves. My old nurse Petale was chained to a block of wood for bringing garlands to my tomb, and Lalage was whipped for daring to stand up for me. Buy them, free them – help them."

I nodded shakily, glancing uncomfortably towards the back of the house, where Lygdamus slumbered peacefully, unaware.

"And burn your poems about me," Cynthia went on, still not satisfied.

"What?!" I cried out, really disturbed now. "Why? You will live on forever in my words!"

"As what?" Cynthia demanded, moving away from me and crossing her bony arms across her singed chest. "As a faithless whore? A flighty nobody you amused yourself with for a while? A pretty but empty-headed thing? No. Burn them – burn them all!"

"But you will be forgotten, when you could have been remembered for a thousand years, two thousand!"

"Give me a simple memorial, like anyone else. I don't need eternal life through poetry, just a stone over my grave that says 'To the divine spirits; here lies Cynthia the Golden.'" She shook the blackened remains of her golden hair in my face, still smarting from where she had struck me two weeks before. She turned away for a moment and said, almost to herself, "I was always faithful to you, you know. Always. I swear it by the Fates themselves. If I'm lying, may vipers break into my grave and swarm over my body, and crush my bones.

"And you," she said, turning back towards me. "*You* will remember me. Look for me in your dreams, the dreams that come through the sacred Gates of Sleep. At night we spirits wander, let loose on the world, free to find those we love and offer them comfort – or not. The great black dog is let out of his cage and he prowls the streets with us, shaking his three heads at the sleeping homes of the living. But as the dawn approaches, he howls, calling us back to him through the night, and we must return to the emptiness below. The ferryman takes us back across the waters of Lethe, the river of forgetting, and we are once again empty shadows without thought or form."

"I will never forget you," I said as she grabbed my chin in her sharp hands again. "I will build you a tombstone and hang it with garlands, I will punish those who killed you, I will burn my verses, and I will be faithful to you and only you for as long as I live!" I made the rash promises in a state of terror at the spectre looming before me with one hand on my chin and the other somewhere even more delicate. I fully intended to keep at least half of them.

But she laughed then, and the laughter was even more terrifying than her anger had been.

"Oh, let some other woman have you for now, if she

wants," she said, darkly, ominously. "Have Phyllis and Teia come over and frolic with them in the garden, or get some other girl – some Lesbia, or a Delia, or a Corinna – and spend what time you can with them, enjoying their living bodies. Kiss their sweet flesh and hold their warm forms, for soon – soon…"

"What?" I rasped.

"Soon, I'll have you," she said, leaning over me, her hands touching my hair so lightly I could barely feel it, staring once more into my eyes. "Soon I alone will hold you. You'll be with me, and bone on ash-stained bone I'll grind."

I tried to reach out to embrace her, but somewhere outside a dog howled. My arms grasped nothing but air, and her shadow slipped away.

FINIS?

A SPANISH WEREWOLF IN ROME

Inspired by Petronius, *Satyricon*, 61-62

Trimalchio, the host of the dinner party, was berating his cook in front of all his guests.

"This pig has not been gutted!" he exclaimed. "Strip the cook to the waist and flog him at once!"

Most of the guests, as well as Trimalchio himself, were former slaves, and they all rushed to the shaking man's defence.

"It could happen to anyone!" they cried. "It was just a mistake! He forgot, he's only human! He will promise not to do it again." Everyone except Encolpius and Ascyltos, the interlopers – posh but broke, they had turned up uninvited in hopes of a free meal. Encolpius' little slave-slash-boyfriend Giton had simpered so nicely that Trimalchio was all for it – he figured such elevated guests could raise him up in society in a way that none of his (immense) riches ever could. They were happy to eat the food, but sneered and snickered at everything else about the party, from the guests, to the hosts, to the art on the walls.

"Well, I suppose you're all right, it could happen to anyone," said Trimalchio, a sly smile playing across his lips. "Since you're so forgetful, Gaius, you'd better gut the pig right here and now – I don't trust you to remember it if you take it all the way back to the kitchen!"

The guests sat back to see what would happen next – all except for Encolpius and Ascyltos, who grimaced and looked horrified. Gaius the cook put his tunic back on, grabbed his knife, and carefully started slicing the pig's belly – at which point, as the skin fell open, hot sausages and black puddings fell out in a delicious-smelling, steaming heap on the tray underneath.

Everyone cheered, even the snobs, and Trimalchio looked very pleased with himself. Gaius was sent away with a silver coin and a cup of wine, and everyone helped themselves to the meat.

"That was a classic, Trimalchio!" exclaimed Niceros, wiping tears of laughter from his eyes.

"And delicious, too!" added Plocamus, through a mouthful of sausage.

"I thank you all," said Trimalchio, half-rising to take a little bow before settling back down to some black pudding. "But you have been very quiet this evening, Niceros," he added. "You used to be far better company at dinner. What happened to you?"

"Oh, nothing," said Niceros absently. "I was just thinking, Trimalchio, that's all. I know that's a foreign concept to you!"

Everyone except the two uptight snobs laughed.

"Well stop it, it's bad for you!" said Trimalchio. "Tell us a story, go on – a true story mind you! Niceros," he explained to the other guests, "has had the most dramatic and exciting life. Weird and wonderful things are always happening to him. Whatever dinner he attends, whatever party he goes to, he always comes back with some tale of drama or scandal or some hilarious anecdote or silly situation."

"I wonder what his story from *this* dinner will be like?" muttered Encolpius to Ascyltos.

"Come on Niceros, entertain me! I've entertained you, now you return the favour!" cried Trimalchio.

"All right," said Niceros, putting on a world-weary sigh. "But I have to tell you, much as it might surprise you, nothing really dramatic has happened to me this week." More laughter.

"I can tell you a good story from longer ago, though, from back when I was a slave still. But I'm not sure I should."

Cries all around of "No!," "Come on!" and "Why not?"

"Well, we've got such learned guests at this party," said Niceros, gesturing to Encolpius and Ascyltos. "I'm afraid they'll laugh at me."

Encolpius and Ascyltos did their best to assure him otherwise, though not very convincingly, their open hands waving around their mouths and barely hiding their smirks. Everyone else, though, begged him to ignore them and to tell his story.

"All right, all right!" said Niceros eventually. "I'll tell the story, and our snobby friends here can laugh at me if they want to, it won't do me any harm. Better to be laughed at with a smile than to be mocked with cruelty, anyway."

And with that he launched into his tale.

*****

"Back when I was a slave, I was based at my master's town house, in a tiny little narrow alley just round the corner from a good pub. The landlord, Terentius, was well off – he was doing good business and ran a farm out in the country too. He also had this lovely little wife, Melissa, her name was. I say little because she was short, but she was a lovely shape – all plump and rounded, such a sexy belly and the tastiest big b- anyway. To be honest, her very pretty looks weren't the really attractive thing about her. She was also just incredibly kind. She shared everything she had, never refused anything, and never cheated on anyone she borrowed from.

Well, as you can probably tell, I fell hopelessly in love with her. It wasn't ever really a sexual thing, I just loved her smile and her big heart, and all I wanted was to be with her all the time.

She and her husband used to spend part of the summer in their country house up at the farm, and I always missed her horribly. Then one summer, while my master was away on business in Capua, word got back to us that the husband had died suddenly. I couldn't bear to think of her suffering all alone – plus it seemed like a pretty good opportunity to get close to her – so I decided I had to go to her straight away (and before my master came back).

Trouble was, their farm was a good step away, I had no horse, and it was the middle of the night (I may have been in the taverna when I heard about the landlord's death). You know what the roads are like at night – there's robbers and bandits behind every tombstone. I had a pretty decent master, and I had no intention of getting stolen and sold on to someone worse, or beaten and robbed and left lying in the street.

I got lucky again, though, because my master had left a guest, an old family friend, staying in the house. He was a soldier, a tough-looking Spanish bloke with big wide shoulders, a couple of just-attractive-enough scars, and some military tattoos. He was incredibly brave – so he told us – and he seemed like the perfect travelling companion-slash-bodyguard. And he was bored enough to be up for the trip, or that's what I figured anyway, when he said yes to a midnight stroll to a farm several miles away to see a woman I fancied and a bunch of chickens.

So we set off. By that time it was the last watch of the night, about two hours after midnight. The full moon was shining so brightly, it was as light as noon. Around about the fifth milestone, he said he had to answer the call of nature. I said yeah, I need to pee too, and we both stopped and hopped behind a couple of tombs to do what we needed to do. I was done after a minute or two and turned to see how my soldier-friend was getting on.

You all might not believe this, but I'm telling you, it was the weirdest thing. He'd stripped off all his clothes and put them in a neatly folded pile by the roadside. Then – not behind the tomb, but in full view of the road – he cocked his leg like a dog and pissed in a big circle all around the pile of clothes. Seriously, I kid you not, that's what he did. So of course I thought, oh Jove, I'm all alone in the middle of the night with a madman.

But it got worse.

It started with his hands. He hunched up on all fours and stretched his hands out in front of him and they... kept stretching. His fingers crept out along the ground, getting longer and bonier until they were claws, and fur started sprouting up all along his wrists and up his arms. Then he sort of thrust his backside up into the air and fur started coming out of his skin all along his buttocks and down the back of his legs. The hair on his chest grew and started to take over his whole body, and flowed up his neck to cover his head, which had been bald only a few minutes before. Then he raised his face up to the sky and I saw that his nose was stretching, pulling out from his face – I could hear the sickening crack of his bones twisting and breaking and growing outwards. His mouth seemed almost to get pulled into his nose, and then he opened it and his teeth were huge and sharp, and he looked up and howled at the moon.

He wasn't a man any more – he was a wolf.

I can hear some of you sniggering. I'm telling you, this is no joke. I'd never lie about it – it was too horrible!

He howled again, and then turned and stared right at me. I was stuck to the spot, frozen in terror. I felt like my actual soul was going to fly out of my body from the sheer fright. Then suddenly he lunged, and I ducked and rolled just in time. As I scrambled through the grass, his teeth got close enough to graze my bare leg, just above the ankle. But I got lucky – a bunch of wild dogs started barking somewhere out in the woods. The wolf howled again and ran off after them.

I managed to peel myself off the ground and go over to look at the pile of clothes he'd left behind. The whole pile had turned to stone! A stray dog wandered up, sniffed a bit at it – where the soldier had pissed all around the pile – and turned around and ran away the minute it got a whiff.

I was terrified, but I was more than halfway to Melissa's house. Luckily I'd thought to bring my iron sword with me, which is obviously the best defence against magical beings, so I drew it and held it at the ready, and just kept on going. I was slow, though. Every time I saw a shadow move I waved my sword at it, slicing into nothing and killing I don't know how many tricks of the light. The moonlight was no help at all, it just made the shadows deeper. I jumped out of my skin if I heard an owl hoot or a mouse rustle around in the grass. I was shaking like a leaf, sweat pouring down my back and running down my legs the whole way.

I finally reached Melissa's house around dawn. She heard me coming – the dogs were barking I think – and came straight out to meet me.

"Niceros! Niceros what's happened to you? You look terrible!" she cried, wrapping her kind arms around me and sitting me down with a cup of hot wine to still my shaking.

"I couldn't possibly tell you," I moaned miserably, spilling the wine all over my tunic.

"Well, whatever it was, it's over now," she said. "Though it's a shame you didn't get here just a little bit earlier, you could have helped us. A wolf got into the yard and attacked the sheep. There was blood everywhere!"

"A wolf?!" I cried.

"Yes, but don't worry. Our overseer was on the case, he put a spear right through its neck!"

They'd murdered the soldier who was staying as a guest in my master's house! If I didn't do something, I figured I and every other slave in the household would be crucified for sure!

I screamed in horror and fled straight back home, leaving Melissa standing, dumbfounded, on her doorstep. I ran faster than I've ever run before, all the miles back to the house. I stopped only once, briefly, to look for where the pile of clothes had turned to stone, but there was nothing there but a pool of blood.

You're all former slaves – most of you – you can imagine my relief when I staggered in to the house, chest aching from breathing so hard, feeling like Pheidippides about to die after running from Marathon, only to find our soldier-guest lying in bed, a great big ox of a man, very much alive, human, and being treated by our local doctor. He had a nasty-looking wound on his neck, but otherwise he seemed fine.

I was very glad he hadn't been murdered and we weren't all going to be crucified, but now I knew for sure we had a skin-changer staying in the house. For the rest of his visit, I couldn't sit down with him or share food or drink with him, I was too terrified. The weird part was, I was never entirely sure whether he really knew what he was or not. He didn't seem at all embarrassed when he saw me, which surely he should have been, when I knew he'd been injured while eating the flesh off living sheep's bones! And he never threatened me or ordered me to keep his secret. Maybe he didn't remember anything about being a wolf? But then, if so, what did he think had happened?

Now, some of you giggling back there might have a different explanation for all this. Fair enough – think whatever you want. But I swear, I'm telling the truth – may your guardian spirits punish me if I'm lying!"

*****

"What a story!" declared Trimalchio happily when Niceros had finished. "If it's true – well, it made my hair stand on end! And of course, it must be true, because I know Niceros never talks nonsense or lets his tongue run away with him!" At this, there was raucous laughter all around the table. Niceros laughed along with the rest, more or less, a bit shakily. He was nervously scratching his leg just above the ankle.

"Now I'll tell you *my* horror story," said Trimalchio, and he launched into a story about a witch and a straw mannequin. Niceros listened and laughed along with the rest, but lapsed back into quiet himself. Encolpius and Ascyltos, the snobby interlopers, continued to snigger behind their hands at everyone and everything around them, while young Giton picked miserably at his food.

After telling his story, Trimalchio decided to have his huge dog, Scylax, brought into the room. One of the younger boys at the table was feeding an overweight puppy, which sent the huge guard dog into a fury; he lunged at the smaller animal and started barking the house down, upsetting several of the more delicate dishes on the table as well. Both animals started running around the room, while the guests looked on with sneers (Encolpius and Ascyltos) or delight (everyone else). Neither animal, despite the chaos, would come anywhere near Niceros, but in all the excitement, no one really noticed that.

After the dogs had been taken out, Niceros took advantage of a lull before the next round of savoury dishes to say that he was tired and would be heading home.

"It's the full moon tomorrow," said Encolpius, leering at him. "Aren't you afraid to be walking home alone at night? Should we send one of Trimalchio's door-guards with you?"

Niceros absent-mindedly scratched behind his ear. "I have nothing to fear tonight," he said. "But if I were you, Encolpius, I'd watch my back tomorrow. And don't be so sceptical about the supernatural. You might need to know this stuff some day."

Encolpius sniggered again. Niceros ignored him and said goodbye to Trimalchio (who was barely paying attention, as he was setting up his next surprise for his guests – an elaborate mock-up of his own funeral complete with a fake skeleton), and he left, the sounds of the party gradually fading into the night behind him. As he walked home alone through the dark and empty streets, Niceros glanced up towards the nearly-full moon and gave out a quiet howl.

FINIS

A TOMB FOR A WEDDING-BED

Inspired by Phlegon of Tralles, *On Marvels*, 1

Machetes checked the address his father had written out for him on his wax tablet. Yes, this was it – the home of his father's old friend from his student days. Where better to study Greek philosophy than Greece itself? Machetes wondered what this Demostratos was like – whether he was dour and serious like his father, or whether perhaps his father really was more playful in his younger days, as his mother kept telling him.

His curiosity had to wait a little longer as the door-slave opened the door, and he was shown in to a small front room. Finally, his host appeared. A small, wiry man, Demostratos seemed very prim and proper. Not as dull, perhaps, as Machetes' father, but not quite the more playful host he was hoping for.

"Greetings," said his host, pleasantly enough, but not warmly. "Welcome to my home." The sentiment was in his words and his gestures, but didn't quite reach his eyes.

"Thank you, sir," said Machetes politely. "It is very kind of you to put me up, and I hope it's no trouble. I intend to stay only a few days."

"No trouble at all, no trouble," said Demostratos in a weary tone that suggested it might be some trouble. "Dinner will be ready very shortly. In the meantime, I'll show you to your room."

"Thank you," said Machetes. "You have a lovely home. Two stories! Very nice."

"We are rather traditional, my wife and I," said Demostratos. "We keep a separate women's quarters upstairs, and men's downstairs. You might perhaps be expecting to see my wife at dinner, but we stick to the old ways. There are no other guests, so it will be just you and I."

"Oh – lovely," said Machetes, his heart sinking. He had been hoping to meet his host's wife, Charito, a lady his father had told him was very beautiful (though he wondered now how his father could possibly have known that). The thought of an entire evening with only this rather uptight man to chat with was not terribly appealing. As they moved through the hall towards the dining room, he thought he heard movement upstairs, and perhaps even spotted the flick of a skirt as it was whisked back up the stairs and away from him, but that was all.

Dinner was as dull as Machetes had feared, and no entertainment had been laid on either. It was just him and Demostratos, discussing philosophy and drinking cheap wine, badly mixed with the wrong amount of water. Several times, Machetes tried to let his host talk and allow his own mind to wander, but Demostratos kept asking him questions, and not simple small-talk questions – really deep philosophical questions. He kept asking things like what Machetes thought about Fate, or Pain, or Why It Rains, and Machetes had to keep his wits about him. He waited until he had eaten enough to be polite and then, though the sky had barely darkened, he made some excuses about having had a long journey and took himself off to his room.

Exhausted, Machetes lay back fully clothed on the bed and listened to the sounds of the household winding itself down for the night. He must have fallen asleep, for he was woken up in full darkness by the sound of someone opening the door and slipping into his room.

"Who's there?" he cried in alarm, fumbling to light the

lamp by the bed.

"Don't worry," said a light, bright voice from the end of the bed. "I won't hurt you."

"Who are you?" He managed to get the lamp lit and held it out in front of him. At the end of the bed stood a young woman. She wore a white dress and simple gold jewellery that suggested good taste, and a decent if not huge amount of money. A single rose was pinned into her dark curly hair, which fell across her face in a way that might have been artful and deliberate, or genuinely carefree – either way, it was as beguiling as she surely wanted it to be.

"My name is Philinnion," she said with a smile, "but be careful, we must be quiet – my parents don't know I'm here."

"Are you Demostratos and Charito's daughter?" hissed Machetes in a horrified whisper. "Yes, please don't tell them you've been here – your father will have my head, he wouldn't even let you or your mother down to dinner!"

"I know," said Philinnion sadly. "He's terribly old-fashioned."

"It's not like that in Rome," said Machetes conversationally. "There, it is the wife's job to help host a dinner, and daughters ready for marriage sometimes come as well."

"I know," said Philinnion eagerly, moving forward to sit down on the bed beside him. "I've read about it in books. Most Greek households are that way these days as well – but my father has this obsession with holding up what he calls 'old-fashioned family values.'"

Machetes chuckled. "He's not what I was expecting. From what my father says, he wasn't always that way. My father is very strict, but he says yours was terribly badly behaved when they were studying together."

Philinnion giggled. "That's what my father says about yours!" she said.

Machetes watched her laugh, feeling the closeness of her sitting beside him on the bed. He started to find himself becoming uncomfortable.

"You had better go," he said. "If your father catches us, I dread to think what he will do to you."

"My father has never allowed me to so much as smile at a man," said Philinnion sadly. "I spent most of my life within these walls, and went out veiled and silent when allowed. And soon my Hades will take me away, and my chance will be gone."

Machetes thought this was a rather flowery and unnecessarily gloomy way to describe getting married, but he supposed it must seem that way to a young girl, being taken away to the house of an older man she barely knew, chosen by her father, for a new life she might not even want. He hesitated, and she put her hand on his upper thigh.

"It's so nice just to sit with you, and talk with you," she said. "I'm enjoying it so much." And she smiled at him again, and his heart melted. He started to pull back once more, but she suddenly leaned across and kissed him full on the mouth, her hands wandering down to his tunic, and he gave up trying to behave himself, and gave in to her.

Afterwards, they lay together on the narrow guest bed, and he twirled his fingers around her hair.

"I want you to have this," she said, taking a golden ring off her finger. "My mother gave it to me, but I want you to have it, to remember me by."

"All right," said Machetes, smiling. "Then you take this to remember me," and he gave her the iron ring from his own finger. "If your husband asks you about it, tell him it was your father's, or your mother's father if you think he won't believe that."

"I will," she said. Playfully, she grabbed the cheap gilded wine-cup lying on the top of his pack. "I should take this as well," she said, "for it suits me!" It had a rather badly done image of Persephone picking flowers on it.

"Take it, it was cheap, I won't miss it," said Machetes. "But now, come back to bed. I'm here for several nights," he took a deep breath, "will I see you again?"

"Of course," she said, and she blew out the lamp and came

back to him.

When Machetes woke in the morning, there was no sign of Philinnion anywhere, but the golden ring lay on the table beside him, and she had carelessly left her breast-band lying on the bed. He sniffed it happily, for it still smelled of her – roses and wine – and he tucked it in to the bottom of his pack before steeling himself to re-join her serious-natured father for breakfast.

*****

Two nights later, Cilissa grumbled to herself as she cleared the dishes from the dining room, hours after the men had finished eating. Perhaps someday there would be another baby in the house for her to nurse, though there seemed little chance of that now. She was grateful to her master and mistress for keeping her on and not selling her to some new family, but her duties were not quite as fulfilling as they had once been.

There was no one else around, so she sat down briefly and nibbled at some of the tastier-looking leftovers. All was quiet in the house – or almost. As she sat still in the growing darkness, she thought she heard someone walking across the room behind her, from the direction of the front door. Cilissa thought she must be hearing things, for who would be coming in at this time of night? The master and mistress had gone to bed; Machetes was the only guest, and he had disappeared to his room as quickly as possible after dinner. But still, she picked up an oil lamp and went to look for the source of the sound, thinking perhaps it was a mouse or a rat that would need evicted, or otherwise got rid of.

Looking around in the shadows, she thought she saw someone moving toward Machetes' room. She held up the lamp and got a decent view of the figure as it made its way towards the guest bedroom door. Cilissa felt her heart skip a beat. She could hardly believe the evidence of her eyes. There, surely, was Philinnion, a rose in her dark hair and her own gold earrings hanging from her ears, slipping into the young man's room!

Cilissa closed her eyes and shook her head.

"I am seeing things," she said to herself. "I am becoming an old woman and I am seeing things!" She went to turn away, but hesitated as she heard the sound of low moaning coming from the guest bedroom.

"No," she changed her mind. "I have to know."

She hurried to the door of the room and opened it quietly. The young lovers were wrapped in each other's arms and completely oblivious to her, but she could clearly see the familiar profile of the young woman. It was definitely Philinnion. Her Philinnion, her baby, the child she'd nursed, comforted, wrangled, and taught, her little girl. She would have known her anywhere. Shaken to the core, she pulled the door closed again just as quietly and hurried upstairs to the women's quarters.

"Madam! Madam!" she hissed, knocking on Charito's door. She heard grumbling from inside. "Madam!" she called again.

"What?" Charito pulled the door open, looking none too happy. She was still dressed, but had taken off half of her jewellery and her face was freshly red from being washed.

"Madam, your daughter – she is alive!" cried the old nurse, grabbing her mistress's hands in delight.

"What are you talking about?" demanded Charito coldly, ripping her hands away.

"Philinnion! I've seen her with my own eyes! She's alive, she's – in the guest's bedroom." Cilissa faltered a little, realising that she did not want to get her charge in trouble.

"Cilissa, you have gone completely mad," said Charito, shaking. "Get out of here at once. We will discuss your behaviour in the morning."

Cilissa drew herself up to her full height and refused to move. "Do I look mad?" she demanded. "Am I out of my wits? Am I spouting nonsense?"

"Since you are telling me that my dead daughter has snuck in to have an affair with our house-guest, yes!" exclaimed

Charito. "Now get out!"

But Cilissa refused to move. "Come with me," she said. "Come with me, and I'll show you it's true."

Charito had not intended to indulge this demand from her slave, but Cilissa was by now talking so loudly that the whole house had been roused, and she could hear Demostratos demanding to know what was going on from downstairs. Still trembling at the mention of her daughter and desperate to put an end to whatever madness this was, she threw a shawl around her shoulders and wordlessly followed the old nurse downstairs to the guest room. As they passed her husband's bedroom, he emerged and opened his mouth – she shook her head briefly and motioned to him to follow them.

The little procession made its way to the guest room, where Cilissa flung open the door and stood back. Charito looked inside, and saw the unmistakeable shape of her daughter lying in the arms of their house-guest. Stunned, she froze to the spot. She was even more astonished to see her calm and reserved husband take one look and rush forward to embrace his little girl. Nothing was said about finding her half-naked in a man's bed. He simply threw his arms around her, and wept into her hair.

Machetes looked appropriately horrified to be caught sleeping with his host's unmarried daughter, but Philinnion looked utterly crushed. Slowly, she pulled apart from her father's embrace. She gave her astonished mother a quick hug, then stood back, tears streaming down her cheeks.

"Mother, Father, why did you come?" she asked, her voice breaking.

Everyone stood in stunned silence for a moment. Machetes opened his mouth as if to say something, but closed it again.

"I prayed to Aphrodite so hard when I was dying," choked Philinnion. "I just wanted to love and to be loved. And then when this wonderful man came to stay with you, at last she granted my prayer!" She turned to smile at Machetes, who managed a weak smile back. "But now," she turned to her parents again, "now everything is ruined, and I have to go back, and you have to say goodbye to me all over again."

And with that, she took one more deep breath, stiffened out into the frame of a corpse, and dropped at their feet.

Charito, Demostratos and Machetes all fell on her at once, weeping and pleading with her to get up and to talk to them. But it was no use. She lay stiff, pale, and cold, her heart not beating, with no breath of life in her. She was clearly dead.

"What have you done to her?" cried Machetes.

"What have *we* done to her?" Charito tore her clothes, ripping her veil from her head and throwing it on the ground, tearing her hair out and drawing her nails down her cheeks. "What have *you* done? Did you raise her from the dead just to torment us?"

"What?" cried Machetes. "Of course not! This girl wasn't dead, she was a living breathing girl until just now!"

"She was dead," said Demostratos in a hollow voice. "She died six months ago. She was our daughter, Philinnion. That is her gold ring, sitting just there," and he pointed to the bedside table.

Machetes shuddered at the mention of her name, but stuck to his story. "It cannot have been your daughter," he said firmly. "It must have been some other girl who looks like her, who stole the ring from her grave. I am telling you, the woman I was with was a living woman!"

"There is one way to resolve this," said Cilissa from the doorway. "We should go to the family mausoleum. If we find Philinnion's body there with the ring missing, we know this girl for some kind of thief or trickster, and we will throw her body to the birds. If Philinnion's body is missing, we will know she was telling the truth and it was really her, and we will bury her once more, with all ceremony. And perhaps we will burn her bones this time."

"You want to go out to the mausoleum now, at this time of night?" demanded Demostratos, but no one else seemed to want to wait. And so, equipped with torches, and with a dog and a door-slave for protection, all four traipsed out of the house and into the night.

*****

The graveyard was not far away, as the family lived near the edge of town, and the moon was out, so the night was bright. No one spoke as they made their way through the streets, the sounds of drunken men outside the tavernas drifting out across the night. Even the dog was quiet, looking up at them all as if to ask why they were taking such a strange walk at such an odd time of night. In a weird parody of a funeral, they carried their torches to the mausoleum, where Demostratos pulled open the door and silently, they trooped inside.

It was a big mausoleum – the family had quite a bit of money in the past. More recent bodies lay on biers around them, the odour fading but still pungent, their forms slowly melting into the stones they lay on. On shelves surrounding them were the bones of older ancestors, jars of ash and bone fragment in row upon row all the way up to the low ceiling. But one bier, the one nearest the door, was empty. Almost empty – for lying on top of it was an iron ring and a cheap wine-cup with a rough image of Persephone on it.

Machetes let out one great cry when he saw them. Then, snatching up the ring, he grabbed a torch and fled from the place.

"It was really her," said Charito, her voice breaking. "It was really her, and we – we spoiled it somehow. We could – we could – could we have had our daughter back?"

She went to Demostratos, who held her silently and they wept together. Cilissa was weeping too, but she tried to find some comfort for them.

"She didn't come back for us," she said. "We couldn't have kept her. She didn't come back for us, and she would have been gone as soon as he was."

"The poor young man," said Demostratos. "He must be quite shaken."

"You feel for him?" said Charito, looking at her husband

in surprise.

Demostratos shrugged his shoulders. "We were all young once," he said, "young and impulsive. And I think it is safe to say *she* came to *him*, since he hardly came seeking her in her tomb."

"We should check on him," said Cilissa. "He has had a nasty shock. And I believe he really loved her, though they did not know each other very long. They seemed truly happy together."

Demostratos and Charito nodded their agreement, and once again the odd little party made their way through the sleeping town. As they came back into the house, they called for their guest, but there was no answer.

"He has probably gone to his room," said Charito, "perhaps we shouldn't disturb him."

"No, we should check on him," said Cilissa, who was starting to feel a pit form in her stomach.

And so they opened the door to the guest room once more. The body of Philinnion still lay stretched out on the floor. Above her hung the body of the young man, dangling from the ceiling, dead. His feet dangled over the remains of his lost love, and on her cold breast he had left two rings, one iron and one gold, and a wax tablet.

"I have gone to join my love," the tablet read. "Farewell."

FINIS

THE WITCH OF THESSALY

Re-told from Lucan, *Civil War*, 6.413-830

Thessaly is a land of sun and shadows, of mountain crags and wide green plains, of thickly wooded forests and neatly planted vineyards. It is the land of the gods, Mount Olympus rising up into the clouds to the north, and it is the land of heroes, as the pass of Thermopylae, the Hot Gates, takes you south to Locri. Above all else, it is the land of witches.

The plants, the herbs, the very rocks of Thessaly can be turned to evil. The gods themselves can do nothing – these witches bend them to their own will using potions and incantations and the secrets of wizards and magicians. They will take the caul from a new-born foal and use it to poison or destroy men's minds; they fill old men with illicit lust and drive hot-headed youths towards loves not intended for them by Fate or Fortune.

They can command the very skies, the very gods, the very universe itself. They can stop the movement of the heavens, and drench the land with unnatural rain. They whip up the sea when there is no wind, they stop the waterfall in its tracks; the Nile does not flood, and Olympus sinks below the clouds. They can draw down the stars and the moon from the sky, and when the moon is dragged into Earth's shadows, she spills out her light as poisonous foam, and the witches gather the tainted grass to mix in their bronze cauldrons.

But Erichtho – she is another type of beast all together. Grasping for the foal or drawing down the stars is too holy, too devout for her. She is mistress of the graves, devoted to Erebus, the god of darkness, and his wife Night, and all the gods of the underworld and the shadows. Her face is haggard and deathly pale, her hair matted and filled with filth.

She lives in abandoned tombs, driving out the ghosts, placing herself near to an abundant supply of her chief requirement: the dead. She steals charred bones and ashes, still smoking, from funeral pyres, carrying off the holy incense as well while she's there. She even gathers the fragments of clothes and strands of hair as they flutter away from the corpse, still smelling of death. She breaks open the body out of the sarcophagus, beating on the dry and preserved bones, gnawing at the yellowed fingernails and scooping out the solidified eyeballs in delight. She takes down the hanging bodies of criminals with her own mouth, chewing at the noose. She scrapes at the remains of the crucified, scratching at the rain-beaten flesh and bones exposed to the sun, and she steals the nails that were driven into their hands, clotted with gore. If a body is left exposed, she waits for the wolves to tear into the flesh, and then steals their treats from their mouths.

She is not always patient enough to wait for a corpse to come her way – she is more than willing to murder the living in order to procure the dead. Some of her spells require the warmth of freshly spilled blood, or the use of still-quivering organs for her ghoulish rituals. And so she slits the throat of a human being like an animal led to sacrifice. Sometimes she buries living souls in tombs, and takes the dead corpse out in a perverted funeral procession. The gods above grant her every prayer at her first asking, for they are afraid to hear a second spell.

*****

It was the night before the battle, and dawn was slow in coming. Camped out by the plain of Pharsalus, the men could see the shadows of the hills around them, and they had heard local rumours of the witch who lived in the dark tombs at their feet.

While most of the men shuddered and turned their backs to the hills, Sextus Pompey, son of the general, was more attracted than repulsed. Sextus did not like camping out in the wilds, he did not like the deserted plains of northern Greece, and he did not like sitting around night after night, waiting for something to happen. Most of all, he did not like uncertainty. Sextus was a planner. He liked to organise himself, his household, his men, and his life, so that nothing came as a surprise, but events always proceeded in a sensible order, to a foregone conclusion. This endless waiting in the Thessalian night was driving his mind to distraction. Any level of uncertainty around what to have for dinner irked him, and now he found himself with no idea whether or not he would still be alive in twenty-four hours' time. The clash between Julius Caesar and Sextus' father Pompey was like no other Rome had ever seen, and none could say which of the two distinguished generals would prevail. And so Sextus waited, and shivered, and rocked back and forth, and groaned, and asked every man around him, "What do you think will happen? What do you think will happen? What do you think? What do you think?" until no one would talk to him, for all the others preferred to turn to wine and women and the warmth of the fire for temporary relief.

At the darkest hour of the night, Sextus picked his way alone across the empty fields towards the tombs. For a while he searched in vain, peering into the depths of a sarcophagus with the lid sitting slightly off, poking around the urns near to fresh grave markers. But then he saw her. Where the cliff jutted out over the graveyard and the mountains sloped down to the plain of Pharsalia, she sat at the top of a cliff, waving her arms to weave a spell.

Breathing heavily, Sextus hauled himself up the rocky slope towards her, and as he came near he could hear her muttering vile incantations. She ordered the gods of the underworld not to break their promise to her; not to move the battle from her fields, but to make sure the Roman dead piled up at her feet across the plain when morning broke. She was hoping that either Caesar, or Pompey, or both of them, would be left in pieces strewn across the battlefield, so she could gather their bones, and master their ghosts.

Sextus approached quietly across the wet grass, almost on tip toe. Suddenly his feet found a stray twig on the ground and it snapped, and the witch's head shot up.

"Oh famed Thessalian!" Sextus declared grandly, before the witch could speak. "You have the power to reveal the future to mortal men, and even, they say, to alter the course of events. Speak to the gods for me, or extract the answers I need from the ghosts and shadows of the underworld. Call Death herself and make her tell me which one of us she will come for tomorrow! I am no ordinary solider, as you may know," and here he puffed himself up a little, "for I am the son of Pompey Magnus, the Great, the leader of the Roman state. After tomorrow, I will be heir to either the whole world, or to immense ruin. And so I pray you, tell me please, what will be the outcome of the battle tomorrow?"

Erichtho pulled her matted hair away from her eyes to peer short-sightedly at the quivering man before her. She sucked on her blackened, gappy teeth and shook her head a little.

"What you ask," she said, "might be easier if you yourself were not quite so exulted." And she made him a little mock bow, and carried on. "If a single man is doomed to die, this craft of magic can change his fate, and the gods can be forced to choose another to suffer and wither away. Or, if someone is destined to live a long life, we can cut it short by the use of secret herbs and potions.

"But sometimes, the chain of events is fixed from the beginning of the world, and all humankind stands beneath a single blow. Then all the Fates are troubled by a single change, and not even the art and skill of our chants and incantations can alter it – in these cases, all the Thessalians will admit that

Fortune is the stronger."

Sextus' shoulders slumped and he turned to walk away, but the witch held up her bony hand and called out in her raspy voice, "Stop! I can still help you. I cannot change your fate, for as you so rightly said, you are no ordinary soldier, and on your fate hangs the fate of the world itself. But if you may be content with foreknowledge, if it is only uncertainty that troubles you, and you wish only to *know* your stars, and not to change them, well then, then I can help you."

"Yes, that is what I asked," said Sextus, his teeth chattering with more than cold in the night air. "I go to battle tomorrow, and the Fates will fall as they may, but this doubt and dread is driving me to distraction. I want to know what will happen – whether I will be master, or slave, or worse."

"Well then, that is easy," said Erichtho, standing up and brushing off her tattered skirts. "There are many places to look for such answers – in the earth, in the sky, in the depths of empty space, in the sea, on the plains, or among the cliffs of the far-off mountains of Rhodope. But we need not travel so far, for already there has been great slaughter of Roman by Roman in this war, right at our very feet. We will simply take a corpse from a Thessalian field, for its still-warm lips will speak clearly, not like the vague ramblings of a shaken shade pulled back to a body whose limbs have been scorched by the sun. Come! We will find one."

Not far away there had been a recent skirmish, and Erichtho, her head wrapped in cloud, picked her way through the bodies thrown out to the mercy of the wolves and the carrion-birds. She knew what she was looking for; a body with complete lungs and an undamaged voice box, that would speak clearly without her needing to strain to understand the garbled words of a mangled throat. She found a young warrior whose heart had been pierced, but who was otherwise whole, and she sunk her hook into his flesh and dragged him across the stones and the rocks, to the hollow beneath the cliffs where she practised her craft.

Sextus stumbled down the narrow cliff path to join her. As

he made his way down, under the shadow of the cliff, the moonlight obscured by the rocks, he felt as if he were descending down to the very depths of Hades. Down, down he scrambled, under the shadows of yew trees whose branches never touched sunlight, into a cave lit only by an eerie greenish glow, a light produced by magic that was not of this world.

Erichtho had dressed for the occasion. She had put on a robe of many colours that once belonged to the Furies themselves, and she had pulled back her hair and tied it with ribbons of vipers.

She began by opening up fresh wounds in the corpse's chest and filling it up with fresh blood, and cleansing the skin of gore with a magical potion. In this concoction were all the most powerful ingredients pulled from the mistakes of Nature – the froth of a rabid dog, the innards of a lynx, the hump of a hyena, and the marrow of a snake-fed stag. The sucking-fish, the dragon's eye, the flying snake of Arabia and the ashes of the Phoenix were all thrown in, and the whole lot was held together by common weeds and her own spit. But her incantation was where her strongest power lay – she screeched out with a cry that sounded barely human, echoing the barking of dogs and the howling of wolves, the cry of the owl and the serpent's hiss.

Then her spell began.

"Oh Furies, you vicious Avengers; oh Chaos, always poised to ruin the world; oh Fates, who hold men's lives in your hands; oh Charon, lord of the Styx, who rows the Shades back to me; oh you Stygian horrors of the underworld, with Pluto your king and Persephone your queen; and most of all, oh Hecate, goddess of witchcraft – hear my prayer! I have consumed human flesh in preparation for our meeting, I have split open the breasts of the pious and washed them in warm brains, I have presented you my victims' heads on a platter – listen, and do as I ask! I am not asking you to return one who has been long dead, someone lurking in the depths of the underworld and accustomed to the dark. No, I ask you to fling back to me a soul still winging his way downwards. Knock him back and send him flying back up to me, here to remain until I release him. Send us this Pompeian fresh from the battlefield, to make his prophecy for Pompey's son!"

She raised her head, and there, standing before her, was the ghost of the unburied corpse at her feet. It stood back, unwilling to go near the body, reluctant to re-enter its former prison. The gaping wound, the ruined flesh, was loathsome, the poor spirit robbed of Death's final gift, which is to die no more.

Erichtho was displeased. She whipped the shade with a live snake and cried out to the underworld gods, "Tisiphone and Megara, do you not hear me? Hounds of Hell, shall I drag you up into the light, if you will not obey my command? And you, Hecate, who paints your face before you visit the gods above, I will show them your true form and forbid you from changing your monstrous looks – you will drag yourself pale and wretched before them. I will shame you all, I will tell them all about the pomegranate seeds that bind Persephone, I will blast your realm, Pluto, with light. And I will call upon Him, whose very name will cause the earth to tremble, who can look the Gorgon in the eye, who lashes the Furies with their own whip and swears by the Styx. Will you now obey me?"

At once, the blood flowed in the lifeless corpse, the vital organs stirred and new life crept through the cold flesh. The body shivered, the muscles contracted, and then suddenly the corpse shot up from the ground and stood before the witch and the quivering man, his mouth gaping open soundlessly. He could only speak when spoken to.

"Speak as I command," said Erichtho, "and I will reward you. If you speak true, I will burn your body on a great pyre, and enchant it so that you can never be dragged up from the underworld again. Your second death will be your final death, and you may sleep in peace. But speak clearly! The gods may enjoy teasing men with riddles, but any man brave enough to consult with the shades deserves certainty. Now speak!"

And the dead man spoke, tears flowing down his pallid face.

"Pulled from the bank of the silent river, I have not yet seen the Fates spinning their dreadful threads. But I did meet with the whole host of the Roman dead on my way down to Pluto's realm, and this is what they told me. Violence and grief stirs the Roman ghosts, and a wicked civil war shatters the peace of the land of the dead. The great Roman spirits are angry – Sulla rails at his patroness Fortune, Scipio and Cato weep for their descendants and Catiline has broken his chains and is rejoicing in the chaos. Pluto, lord of the underworld, has thrown open his kingdom; he sharpens broken rocks and hard steel for shackles, and prepares his punishment for Caesar.

"Sextus Pompey, take comfort in this. The dead are preparing to welcome your father and his house to a place of peace, in the brightest part of that gloomy world. Do not be troubled by Caesar's glory, for it is to be short-lived. The time will come, and come soon, that makes all the generals equal. Go forth, and die! Hurry down to the shadows and when you get there, trample on the ghosts of the gods of Rome. The generals' battle determines only their place of burial, whether it will be by the Nile or the Tiber. It is the same Fate, either way.

"Do not ask me your own fate, Sextus Pompey. Your house is divided, and you must fear Europe, Africa, and Asia. Fortune has divided your graves across all three!"

And with that, the corpse fell silent, and stood patiently waiting to die again.

Sextus was an unhappy customer. Several times he tried to persuade the ghost to speak again, to answer his question more clearly, to give him precise information about the battle that would come in the morning. But it was no use.

Erichtho pointed to the mouth of the cave, where the first signs of dawn were creeping over the horizon. "You will get your answer soon enough, son of Pompey," she said. "Don't you understand, you can discover the future without going to so much trouble as this. It will always come to you eventually! And anyway, this good soldier gave you the information you wanted. You wanted certainty, and you have it. It may or may not be this day, but one day soon, you will all certainly die."

Sextus would have protested, but as light crept around the edges of the cave, he saw evidence of the witch's work – scattered bones and cups of poison, bats' wings and sharp knives. He knew of her reputation, and found that, though he might die that day, he did not want it to be here, alone in the darkness with the witch and the corpse.

And so Erichtho got to work once more, and prepared her potions. Together, she and Sextus built a large pyre, and the corpse willingly climbed on top of it. Finally, the dead man's soul was returned to the peaceful river-bank of the Lethe, the river of forgetting, and his body crumbled into ashes.

The witch walked the soldier back to his camp, and there she left him, to face the uncertainty of the day knowing only one thing. By evening, many of those around him would be dead.

FINIS

THE FAULT IN OURSELVES

Inspired by Plutarch, *Brutus*, 36 and 48 and *Caesar*, 69

"What is the best kind of death?" Lepidus asks Caesar on the 14th March.

"The unexpected kind," Caesar replies.

At that same moment, Brutus is reading his own treatise, *Concerning Duty*, by lamplight. He has written at great length about the duty owed by sons to their fathers, and by friends to their friends. He screws up the papyrus and throws it onto the fire.

Morning comes, a spring breeze on the air.

"Don't go," Calpurnia says suddenly, as Caesar prepares to leave the house. "I had a terrible dream last night. I saw your body, streaming with blood, and then I saw the roof of our house collapse. Don't go today! Stay here and lock the door!"

"Don't be daft, woman," says Caesar gruffly, and he dismisses his bodyguard and strides out into the street.

Brutus and Cassius are approaching together, from the opposite direction to Caesar.

"Do you remember what you said about Pompey, once?" Cassius asks Brutus. "You said it was not possible to live as slaves to a lawless king."

"I am not sure it's possible to live under any king," says Brutus. "Any king becomes the master, and we become the slaves. We must live free, or die trying."

"Or both," says Cassius.

"I told you to beware the Ides of March!" the soothsayer shouts at Caesar as he passes.

"And here they are; the Ides have come," says Caesar, "and here I still am, too."

"They have come, but they have not yet gone, Caesar," replies the soothsayer.

Brutus sees Caesar entering the meeting-place, sees Trebonius grabbing onto loyal Antony's arm and keeping him outside. Brutus has strictly forbidden Cassius and the others from unnecessary bloodshed, and Antony will survive this morning. Antony, Caesar's friend, his confidante. His loyal lap-dog. His slave. Brutus will not be Antony. Does not want to be Antony. Did he once want to be Antony? No – never. He follows Cassius inside.

Caesar glances up at the statue of Pompey as he comes into the meeting. A series of images flash through his mind – an angry face in the Senate – a grim face on the opposing side of a battlefield – a bloody, disembodied head in a box. He carries on walking towards the statue.

Tullius Cimber is approaching Caesar, begging for his brother to be allowed back from exile. More men crowd around him – supporting him? Bustling to take their turn next? The crowd becomes rowdy, more like the mob than a group of stately senators.

Tullius pulls Caesar's toga down from the shoulders. Cassius grabs Caesar's face and jerks it towards the statue of Pompey; Caesar has no choice but to stare at the cold marble head as Casca draws a dagger and plunges it into his shoulder.

Caesar grabs Casca's wrist where it holds the blade and

drags his stylus down Casca's arm, red blood pouring from both. But Casca is not alone; from every side, knives appear and for every three that Caesar dodges, a fourth finds its mark.

Caesar bends over at the foot of Pompey's statue, blood pouring from his many wounds, spattering all over the white folds of his toga. Still he stands, almost, hands raised to defend himself. And Brutus steps through the crowd, knife in hand. Something goes out of Caesar then. His shoulders drop, his legs buckle and he falls to the floor.

He is almost done, but not quite yet. "And you, child!" he says in Greek. They can all finish the proverb – "And you, child, will taste this too." Or is it a question? Does it have another meaning for Brutus alone? He will not think it, will not acknowledge it. No matter – no time for that now. The deed has to be done. Is already done. It just needs to be finished.

Brutus strikes.

Caesar pulls the tattered remnants of his toga over his bloodied head and sinks to the ground. The statue of Pompey looms over him, impassive. The senators melt away as Antony's running footsteps are heard approaching.

Brutus looks down at his own bloodied hands.

"Kill Antony!" cries Cassius, and others take up the call.

"No!" cries Brutus. "The blood of one Roman on our hands is enough! And Antony may yet join us." He throws off his bloodied toga and runs to the Capitol to speak to the people. The people will understand. They will be happy, they will be grateful. They will understand, he tells himself. They will understand…

*****

Brutus paced his tent, restless, flipping a coin over and over in his hand. One one side, it showed his own head; on the other, two daggers flanking a freedman's cap and the inscription, 'The Ides of March.' The top of the cap had been worn away by his anxious thumb. Around him, the snoring sounds of the sleeping camp blended into the wind.

"We are free," he murmured to himself, as he had done every night for more than two years. "We are free, now."

He scrutinised the map by the dying lamplight. It would be a long march from here in Sardis to Philippi, re-named for Alexander the Great's even greater father. There was a plain west of the city which would suit them. He had heard that there were some ancient rock carvings not far away, showing horsemen and weapons. Perhaps he would have time to go and see them.

He heard footsteps outside the tent. It was not yet time for the watchmen to come and update him, and Cassius usually slept well no matter what the circumstances – so who was it?

There was a rustling sound. The entrance to the tent flapped open almost of its own accord, and in came a huge, hulking shadow of a man. It moved to stand silently in front of him, the deep shadows on its angular face looking like great black holes. The nose looked almost like Caesar's; then it turned slightly another way, and it looked almost like his own.

The figure struck terror deep inside him. But it simply stood there silently, and did nothing.

"Come on, man!" Brutus said to himself. "Why be frightened of something that shows no desire to do you harm?" Forcing his rational brain to take control of his quivering lips, he asked it, "Who are you? And what do you want with me?"

"I am your evil spirit, Brutus," the thing said in a rasping voice. It held up a hand and gestured towards the map. "You will see me at Philippi."

"I will see you," Brutus told it, and the thing turned and moved out of the tent.

Brutus shook himself hard. He called all the slaves and all the guards into his tent one by one and and questioned them, but all of them, quaking, claimed to have seen and heard nothing. The sky was lightening with the first signs of dawn, so Brutus went to Cassius's tent and shook him awake.

"What do you think it was?" he demanded, after a brief description.

"I think it was your imagination, Brutus," said Cassius grumpily, rubbing sleep out of his eyes.

"I am not in the habit of imagining strange men wandering about my tent," Brutus replied crossly.

"Look," said Cassius, "we can only perceive the world through our senses, correct? And our senses are fallible, and easily deceived. An impression on the senses is like an impression in wax. The soul is like the wax, and it reshapes the impressions as they hit it."

"The soul is like wax?" Brutus said, frowning.

"Yes! I mean, the soul is like a collection of atoms distributed all around our bodies, and as sights or sounds or other senses hit those atoms, the atoms rearrange themselves. Like dreams, when the imagination produces all sorts of things from vaguely remembered impressions. And when your body is worn out, stressed, and overwhelmed, the imagination can run riot."

"I think it was my evil Fate," said Brutus. "I think my Fortune has always been bad, and now it is finally catching up to me."

"The fault, dear Brutus, is not in our stars, but in ourselves," said Cassius. "Besides, I do not believe there is any such thing as an evil Fate, or a divine entity attached to each man's being. Even if such a thing existed, it would not have the appearance or speech of a man. You need to try to get more sleep, my friend. Perhaps you *were* asleep at last, and it was a dream?"

"I was not asleep, and it was not a dream," said Brutus.

"Well, see if you can call it back again," said Cassius with a yawn, calling his slave for a cup of posca. He threw the vinegary mixture down his throat, shivered involuntarily, shook the sleep out of his eyes, and called for another. "If we can convince the men that the gods are on our side, our chances will be much better."

"Did you listen to anything I said?" demanded Brutus in

confusion. "It was not a friendly spirit, whatever it was! It almost looked like Caesar from some angles…"

But Cassius was no longer listening, and Brutus gave it up and returned to his tent.

*****

Three months later, another night, another tent. Whether Philippi was as impressive or as interesting as he had hoped, Brutus could hardly say. All his thoughts were consumed with the plain where Cassius had fought Antony, and had died.

"Sir! Look at this!" One of his men ducked into the tent, waving a cheap pamphlet at him. Produced by Antony and Octavian, it urged all his soldiers to leave him and to join them, the clear victors, the avengers of Julius Caesar.

"Amyntas and his men have already gone over to the Avengers, sir," said the man, standing well back from his general as he spoke. "Why do we delay? The men are keen to end this, one way or the other."

"And are the men leading this army, or am I?" snapped Brutus. He waved the man away.

A new coin was in his hand, and he ran it through and through his fingers, rubbing it with his thumb. Not one of his own: this one showed on one side, Antony, and on the other side, the child Octavian, who was now calling himself "Caesar." The boy had given himself a tiny scrap of a beard in the Greek style in his portrait, a rather pathetic attempt to make his twenty years seem like more. How was this kid Julius Caesar's heir? Three wives, at least three other notable female partners and no doubt dozens more less well known, and somehow Rome's most notorious lover of everything that moved had left only an Egyptian baby and an upstart great-nephew to succeed him.

At least three notable female partners, including Brutus' own mother… Who was this precocious teenager, this non-entity, the spawn of Caesar's niece, to take the name Caesar for himself? He knew nothing of Caesar – or he knew Caesar too intimately by half, according to the rumours. Brutus did not believe that. Caesar was no Greek, to be lured in by a teenage boy. He rubbed the tiny beard on the boy's golden face again, shakily. Rule by a lawless king is the worst kind of rule, Plato said. Rule by a philosopher-king might be the best. He had never really considered the obvious course, that instead of freeing Rome, he could have enslaved them all himself, and with a much better claim to do so than this child.

And Antony. If he had allowed Cassius to kill Antony in Rome... sixty of them, versus one of him. They could have seized power then and there, and he could have taken the name of Caesar, and Rome would be enslaved but happy, and Cassius would be alive.

Brutus wished he could share the Stoics' confidence in the idea that a man's Fate was fixed and immoveable. It was such a wonderful way of avoiding responsibility for anything. It wasn't his fault – he was Fated to save Antony's life that day in March, just as he was Fated to murder his mother's lover. Caesar probably knew that, and that was why he named this spotty boy barely out of his teens as his heir, with Brutus' own cousin as a second, and Brutus himself cast aside. And Cassius had been Fated to die here – that's why the gods made it seem to him as though Brutus had lost his own fight, even as Brutus himself was chasing down the cowardly upstart where the weakling was apparently puking his guts out in the marshes.

As if in answer to his question, he heard footsteps outside the tent and the rustling of the opening coming apart by itself again.

It was back.

The phantom, whatever it was, stood looming over him as before. Its face was impassive, the shadows even deeper than before, its expression just as grim. It said nothing.

"My evil Fate," murmured Brutus. "Have you followed me all my life, spirit? Was I always destined to come to this end?"

Silence.

And then, "The fault is not in our stars, but in ourselves," he heard Cassius saying in his head.

Suddenly, he saw each decision clearly. He chose to kill Caesar, knowing how much Caesar loved him, knowing, perhaps, what he himself meant to Caesar. He did it to save Rome. Had he failed? Not yet, not while he still breathed. He left Antony alive that day – naïve, perhaps, as Cicero had said – poor Cicero! Another death on his conscience. Kill Antony that day in March, and Cicero lives, Cassius lives, perhaps the boy-king Octavian dies, Brutus lives…

But he had done the right thing. The ethical thing. He knew his actions were just. He was a Liberator – he was not a murderer.

He looked up once more at the phantom, and now that strong nose looked almost like Antony. It seemed to flicker in the lamplight, now becoming Caesar again, now Antony, now himself. The three of them, bound up together in blood and ambition and regret.

"The fault is in myself," said Brutus aloud. "But I can find no fault. I regret nothing. I would choose the same again. You can tell that to the sick child who wants to kill me, I care nothing for him. Either Antony or I will come out of this, and if it is him, and not me, then so be it."

He drew himself up to face the phantom head on. Still, it was silent.

"It will be him or me," Brutus said again. But he knew, and the phantom knew, and probably Antony also knew, which of them would die tomorrow.

Brutus squared his shoulders and marched out of his tent. They would fight in the morning.

FINIS

OF BLOOD AND GODS

Inspired by Suetonius, *Augustus*, 6

Another scream echoed down the halls to where Octavius sat in his father's study, pacing impatiently.

"I have to go!" he muttered to his secretary, edging fitfully towards the door.

"I'm sure your wife will understand, master," said the secretary in what he hoped was a soothing tone. "There's no way of knowing how much longer it will be. You could go, hear the debate, and come back, and things could still be the same."

Another scream, almost a groan all mixed up with a long cry of pain, bounced off the walls and sank into the air around Octavius.

"If it was normal business, I wouldn't worry about it," said Octavius for the tenth time that morning. "But Cicero is insisting that he's uncovered this great conspiracy and the whole place is in uproar – he's threatening to execute senators without trial, it's all an enormous mess."

"I'm sure your wife will understand how important it is, master," said the secretary again, working to keep any sense of weariness out of his voice.

There was another scream.

Octavius marched out of his father's study and into the atrium, and started towards the front door of the house, but then paused. He stood next to the pool and turned back and forth several times, now to the front door, now to the courtyard and, behind it, the bedrooms.

Another scream floated across the warm air of the courtyard towards them.

"I'll just go and see, you know – how it's going," said Octavius, turning around and starting to move towards the courtyard.

"What do you mean, master?" cried his secretary in alarm. "There are no men on that side of the house today!"

"Well, you never know, there might be one any minute now!" said Octavius, trying to sound light-hearted, but it went right over his secretary's head. "I won't go in, I'll just… just… see what's going on," he said vaguely, and he hurried across the courtyard and down the corridor to the bedrooms before he could change his mind.

Atia was not where he expected her to be, in their own bedrooms, but her screams guided him even further into the house, to a tiny room near the slaves' quarters. He wondered why on earth they had moved her in there, but decided the less he knew about the whole process, the better. He was close enough now to hear words in the screams. Mostly it was repeated cries of, "I can't do it, I can't do it," and at one point, alarmingly, "I think it's stopping, I'm fine, really, it's not going to be today, I'm going to go and get a cup of wine." Thankfully, he could hear the midwife firmly putting a stop to that idea.

Octavius pressed himself against the wall of the corridor with the idea that as soon as a slave-girl came past to get towels or hot water or something (weren't those the usual requirements?), he would stop her and ask her what was going on, and how long she thought it was likely to take.

The screams had started again, even louder and longer now. The midwife seemed to be ordering Atia to do something over and over again, but he wasn't sure what.

Then suddenly, and quite clearly, he heard Atia yelling for all she was worth, "I'm tearing apart! Everything's coming apart! I can see my guts floating up to the stars and spreading themselves over the entire earth and the heavens!" For a moment he was really worried, but then he heard the reassuring voice of the midwife saying something in soothing tones, and decided it was probably all right.

"It's an omen!" he heard one of the slave girls whisper as they hovered by the door of the room.

"An omen of what? That she's going to die?" asked another.

"Don't be so literal!" said the first. "It's an omen that the baby will come out of her and rule over the whole world and the heavens above!"

The second slave girl laughed. "Well, if you say so!" she said. "Though I doubt too many babies born in teensy little back bedrooms are going to do that!"

At that point, the midwife called them back. It sounded as if things were happening; Octavius decided to go back to wait in his father's study. If the Senate were making history, they would have to do it without him, at least for another half an hour.

He wondered briefly as he walked back down the hall whether the superstitious slave girl might be right. Of course not, he told himself, don't be ridiculous.

But as he crossed the courtyard and passed a small statue of Apollo in the garden, the strangest feeling came over him. He found himself shaking as if he were sick, and he had to pause for a moment to catch his breath. He had a sudden strange conviction that not only would the slave girl's prediction turn out to be right, but that he would not live to see it. But he could see his secretary waiting for him, and he pulled himself upright and carried on. Still, although his bedroom was too far away to hear the baby boy's cries from his little nursery, and the child was firmly in the care of the women, Octavius would get no sleep that night.

*****

"You are the man of the house now, Gaius Octavius Thurinus," said the little boy's nurse solemnly, "so you must be a big, brave boy and sleep alone at night."

"But it's scary!" protested the four-year-old, clutching his favourite blanket. "I don't like it here. It's dark and it's cold. It's not as nice as my other bedroom. I want to go home!"

"Nonsense!" said the nurse as harshly as she dared. "You were born in this room, you know, so you are hardly going to come to any harm from sleeping here. You are a big grown-up boy these days, and you will be fine!" And with that, she shut the door and left the little boy, still wearing his black tunic from his father's funeral, sitting alone on the bed in the tiny room, clutching and chewing at his blanket.

Thurinus stared at the doorway in the darkness. The room was tiny, much smaller than his room at their house in Rome. The walls felt like they were too close, and it made him feel stuck, like an animal trapped in a cage. There was one tiny window, high up on the wall, and only the smallest sliver of moonlight could get through to him. At first everything just looked black, but then he realised he could almost see shapes in the darkness – the doorway, the table, the outline of the bed frame. He cried, not loudly for someone to come, but quietly, because he missed his daddy. The salty tears fell on the blanket and made it wet and scratchy, but he carried on holding it tight anyway.

He curled up on the hard mattress, facing towards the wall, and was almost falling asleep when suddenly he was thrown violently out of the bed. He landed hard on the floor, tangled in his blanket.

Of course, little Thurinus cried out and began to wail. His mother and his nurse heard the commotion and came to check on him, but when he told them what had happened, they wouldn't believe him.

"Don't tell stories, Thurinus!" said his mother sternly.

"Listen to your mother, child!" said his nurse. "You remember what Aesop said? About the boy who cried wolf?"

"Not a wolf!" pleaded Thurinus. "I don't know what it

was! Something pushed me out of bed!"

But neither woman wanted to hear it, and they told him good-night and firmly shut the door.

Thurinus lay back down in his bed and stared at the ceiling for a while. It was even more difficult to sleep now, but he knew he had to try, so he closed his eyes tight and pulled his blanket over his head. It was almost working when once again, suddenly, with no warning, he was lifted up and thrown out of the bed. It felt like half a dozen invisible hands had grabbed him and were flinging him to the floor, his blanket tangled around his legs.

Thurinus burst into tears, but this time, no one came. He shouted and screamed and threw himself at the door, but nothing. Not even the dogs came to check on him. Terrified, he crawled under the bed, clinging to his blanket, and squeezed his eyes tight shut.

After a little while, he felt movement above him. It was like a wind sweeping across the room, but he huddled as tight as he could against the wall underneath the bed, holding his blanket in front of him like a shield.

As his eyes got used to the darkness, he started to see shapes moving about in the gloom. Feet – it was men's feet, feet poking out from the bottom of togas, at least three pairs of them, and a woman's feet as well, wearing jewelled sandals under a rich red dress. He watched them move to and fro around the room, letting the pitter patter of their criss-crossing footsteps lull him into a sense of rhythmic relaxation, and then –

– a head appeared, on the floor, staring straight at him. It was not attached to a body. Two hands fell from above and flopped either side of it, their bloody stumps showing where they had been removed from their arms.

"There you are!" said the head. "The little boy who finally brought me down! Many others tried but only you, little brat, succeeded!"

"Don't let him take all the credit!" cried a booming voice from above. Thurinus saw another pair of men's feet stop and stand facing towards the head. "It was *me* did this to you, you bleating little weasel, don't pin it on the boy!" The owner of the feet then leaned down to peer at Thurinus under the bed. This one's head remained reassuringly attached to his body, though a stream of blood was running down his leg. "You did for me though, didn't you, you little squirt?" he said, "Or rather, your mate Agrippa did. After Hirtius and Pansa, you lost the taste for doing your dirty work yourself." Two more pairs of feet paused to join the crowd in front of the bed, but their owners remained standing.

Tears streamed down Thurinus' face but he didn't cry out any more. He didn't know why these men were hounding him, but as long as he stayed pressed against the wall under the bed, his blanket in front of him, it seemed like they were too lazy to reach right under and get him. He was afraid that if he screamed or cried, they wouldn't like the noise and they would try to grab him again.

The woman heard his muffled snuffling, though. She shoved the disembodied head and hands roughly out of the way and lay herself down on the floor alongside the bed to stare right into Thurinus' face. She was horribly thin and bony, and her face was gaunt and grey.

"Is this why you couldn't be a better father to me, Papa?" she asked plaintively. "Was it because your own father died? You didn't know how? Is that why you sent me away? He killed me you know – your step-son. He stopped sending me food and he left me to starve. He did what you wanted to do but couldn't quite manage. You knew he would. You knew him. You knew me. You were just too much of a coward to go through with it yourself."

Her bony hand started to inch forward, creeping along the floor like a spider, moving under the bed, reaching out for Thurinus' blanket...

A new pair of feet appeared. They too were covered in blood shining red and sticky, but somehow the bloodstains seemed to glow and empower them. They kicked the woman's hand away and came to stand between Thurinus and the all the other milling, pacing feet.

"Too scared to confront my grown son, are you? You had to come and torment a little boy?" it sneered with contempt.

"Daddy?" said Thurinus quietly, not daring to hope. But when the glossy red-covered toga moved downwards and the blood-spattered face (still attached to the neck, good) looked in towards him, it wasn't Thurinus' daddy – weirdly, it looked a lot like his great-uncle Julius.

"I'm not your daddy, son," said the face of Uncle Julius. "You daddy loves you very much, but he can't reach you from where he is. These people," and he swept his arm up towards the owners of the feet, "these people will be very angry with you one day, but by then you will be too powerful for them. So the cowards have come all the way back here, now, to torture you instead. But I am your second father, and I am more powerful than any of them." And with that, with one more sweep of his arm, he emptied the room – of himself as well as the wretched, pacing feet.

Thurinus stayed where he was all night, until his nurse found him cowering under the bed in the morning. He told her everything, but predictably, she just said it was a nightmare.

"Uncle Julius said they were mad at me," said the boy.

"Yes, dear," said his nurse. "That sort of thing often happens in bad dreams."

"I'm mad at them, now," said the boy.

"Of course, dear," said his nurse absent-mindedly.

"I'm *really* mad at them," said the boy.

The nurse nodded.

"One day I'll hurt them," said Thurinus, remembering the torn wrists, the bloody legs, the bony hand.

"That's nice, dear," said his nurse, not listening.

*****

"And this was the Divine Emperor Augustus' nursery when he was very young," said the enslaved housekeeper Marcus had inherited along with the house when he bought it, whose name was Melitta. "Back then, he was known as Thurinus, because his father won a victory over runaway slaves near Thurii. My parents and grandparents have all been slaves of this house, and we know all its old quirks and traditions," she added proudly.

"If you do a good job, I'll free you and you can run the household as my freedwoman," said Marcus absent-mindedly as he poked around the tiny room. Melitta betrayed no outward sign of emotion at this; inwardly, her heart skipped a beat and she watched her new master intently, trying to assess how honest he seemed to be.

"What has the room been used for lately?" asked Marcus.

"Mostly, we show people around it," said Melitta. "They pay a few coins, and we usually make sure there's a child's bed and a few toys placed in here. Everyone who enters carries out a ritual purification first, to appease the spirit of the Divine Augustus."

"Really?" said Marcus. "How extraordinary. I haven't heard of anyone doing that around the Imperial palaces in Rome."

"Yes, well," said Melitta uncomfortably, shuffling her feet. "This room is a bit different."

"How so?" asked Marcus.

Melitta took a deep breath. Nothing for it but to tell him, he would find out for himself soon enough anyway.

"Anyone who doesn't perform a ritual purification first finds themselves shuddering and seized with terror as soon as they enter the room," she said, shivering a little to prove her point. "No one has spent the night in here in years, for fear of the spirits that haunt this place. It's where the Divine Augustus was born, you know."

"The Divine Augustus was born at the Ox-Heads on the Palatine Hill in Rome," said Marcus, and Melitta bit her lip and fought the urge to correct him. "This room is a bit small, but it would make a decent guest room for someone planning a short stay. We can still allow the curious to come and look around it when it's not otherwise in use."

"Yes, master," said Melitta.

"You're not convinced, are you?" said Marcus, a bit surprised, as the woman had not seemed to be the superstitious type until now. Melitta remained silent for a moment, racking her brains for a safe reply. "I tell you what," said Marcus before she had managed to come up with anything, "*I'll* sleep in here tonight. Then you'll see that there's no reason this shouldn't be used as a guest room. I have a lot of relatives wanting to come and see this place! If you start telling them the Divine Augustus was actually born here, they'll be even more desperate to stay the night!"

"Yes, master," said Melitta. "Will you be carrying out the ritual purification before going to bed?"

Marcus rolled his eyes. "Yes, yes I will, if it will make you feel better," he said.

Marcus had the house slaves set up a small folding bed in the tiny former nursery so he could sleep there that night. It really was very small, but he was committed to the idea of using it as a guest room now, and too determined to back down. Before going to bed, he carried out a brief purification ritual. Melitta still seemed nervous as she checked everything was in order before going to bed herself, but the ritual seemed to offer her some reassurance at least. Rolling his eyes at the silly superstitions of slaves and women – slave women being, therefore, the most superstitious of all – Marcus made himself as comfortable as possible on the rough camp bed and closed his eyes to sleep.

He had barely closed his eyes, when he felt a sensation as if several pairs of hands were pulling at him, and he was thrown out of the bed along with all his bedclothes.

Marcus raised his head from where he now lay on the floor by the door. He was utterly baffled. He could only imagine that he'd had some kind of nightmare, and thrown himself out of bed in a panic at something in the dream. He could still feel the imprint of the invisible hands on his body, but that must surely be his imagination.

He clambered back into the bed and went back to sleep.

It happened again.

Again, the feeling of multiple pairs of hands grabbing at him. Again, he was thrown right across the room to land in a heap in front of the door, tangled up in his own bedclothes.

Marcus shook himself, gathered up the bedclothes, and stood up. He shuddered, as if someone was walking over his tomb. But he was convinced he must just be having violent nightmares, so he made up the bed again and got back in, and closed his eyes tight to try to go back to sleep.

It happened again.

Invisible hands grabbing at him, angry voices (mostly male, one female), a wet feeling on some of the parts of his body they were touching, a sensation of being hurled across the tiny room. Then the impact of his body hitting the door, the bedclothes landing on his face, suffocating him. He pulled frantically at them, straining to see past the rough wool in the dark. He could just make out shapes in the gloom, people walking about, into and through (through?) each other in the cramped space.

"I – I did the ritual!" he blurted out desperately. "The purification ritual!"

He heard a woman's laughter coming from somewhere. "Oh yes, he was always very keen on purification!" The laughter went on and on, with the hard edge of laughter that's only a heartbeat away from desperate, angry tears.

"It's not you that needs purified," said a booming male voice. "You are just in," – and here Marcus felt someone kick him hard in the guts, " – the – way!"

Marcus curled himself into a ball around his aching belly and listened to the rustling sound of people moving around and around in tiny circles. Something stirred in his hair as it poked out from under the bedclothes, and he realised a wind was whipping up and swirling around the room. There were no drafts, and he had no idea where it was coming from, but it seemed to sweep the bustling feet and stalking shadows away. Marcus thought perhaps it was some guardian spirit come to rescue him, but it continued to swirl around him, a cold, biting wind, prickling and niggling and picking at him. At one point he thought he heard a voice whisper, "Why make me a god and then invade my home?" and then the wind got even stronger. This went on for the rest of the night. Marcus pulled the bedclothes over his head, buried his face in his hands, and pressed himself against the door.

That was how Melitta found him the next morning, half-dead in front of the door, tangled up in his bedspread, moaning and muttering and shivering.

"Shut up that room," he said hoarsely.

"Should we let visitors look at it, master?" asked Melitta.

"Let them if they want to," Marcus replied, "but tell them they enter that room at their own risk. I will never set foot in here again."

FINIS

HOME

Inspired by Tacitus, *Annals*, 11.20-21 and Pliny, *Letters*, 7.27

Adrumetum, Africa Proconsularis, 23 CE

The large villa that would house the quaestor and his staff sat amid a grove of palm trees, overlooking the sea. The quaestor himself had a bedroom with a view out over the beach. The junior staff were housed facing the street, but the rooms were clean, and pleasant enough. The courtyard was raised a little, so that as you walked along the colonnade, you could just about see the sand and the sea.

Curtius Rufus was lodged in a room next to Nasidienus, which was just his typical bad luck. The whole time they were on board ship making their way to Africa, he had found Nasidienus standing on corners of the deck or huddled under a sail, gossiping with the captain, the sailors, even the slaves if he could find no one else. And he was mostly gossiping about Curtius Rufus.

One particularly miserable evening, when the wind was up and the sea was choppy, Rufus had come out on deck and stood near the prow, hoping the touch of the breeze on his face would chase away the sickness in the pit of his stomach. He was running his hands through his thick, dark hair, enjoying the feel of the sea spray on his neck, when he heard a voice carried across the deck by the wind.

"Look at that!" the unmistakably nasal voice of Nasidienus was saying. "Rufus, he claims to be, after his 'father.' You know, I knew his father. The man had a head of rich red hair to rival a Celt. You don't see that on *him*, do you?"

"Well, that's true," said another, more conciliatory voice that Rufus did not recognise. "But I've always noticed that red hair tends to go with rather pale skin, so it's hardly surprising. Rufus's skin is much darker than any red-head I've ever seen."

"Exactly!" exclaimed Nasidienus, triumphantly. "Look at the colour of his skin! The man's so dark, he's practically an Ethiopian!"

"What are you getting at, Nasidienus?" said the second voice wearily.

"There are rumours," said Nasidienus darkly. He left a pause, but when his companion declined to show any interest in knowing what they were, he carried on anyway. "His mother – she died a long time ago – she was a rebellious sort. Never got on well with the father, who was already old by the time they were married."

"So I suppose you are suggesting the mother had an affair?"

"Not just any affair," said Nasidienus. "The rumour is, that Rufus' natural father was a *gladiator*."

The ship lurched and Nasidienus' companion suggested they return to their cabins, but Nasidienus was in full flow and would not be stopped.

"The mother used to hang around the gladiators' barracks, they say. There was one slave in particular, an Ethiopian, that she was apparently *very* fond of. After Rufus was born, she used to take him as an infant to the Games and hold him aloft whenever this man was fighting, so that he could see his child."

"Really, Nasidienus," said the other man, "this does not sound very likely. Why would Curtius Rufus Senior have raised the child if the wife was as indiscreet as all that?"

Rufus kept his gaze firmly out to sea, but he could almost

feel Nasidienus shrug in response before carrying on. "The man had no other heir," he said, "I suppose he thought he might as well raise his wife's bastard child as anyone else. Why adopt when she'd presented him with a potential heir right there? He was never very interested in women, anyway. The mother died giving birth to a second, the baby didn't survive either, and Rufus Senior died not long after that, so Rufus over there was raised by his maternal aunt and uncle. I suppose they cared more that he was the mother's son than the father's."

Nasidienus' companion finally persuaded him back inside, but Rufus stayed out on deck, blinking back tears hidden by the rain and the shadows.

He did not know why he let it upset him. He had heard all these rumours before, many times – from the other boys at school, from his cousins, from his aunt's friends when they thought she was out of earshot. His aunt and uncle had always brushed the rumours aside and told him to pay them no mind, but that was a lot easier for them to do than for him. Any time he went anywhere with his family, his darker skin tone and thick, dark hair was noticed. Sometimes, it was a flattering notice – more than one young woman had batted her eyelids at him and smiled slyly, clearly finding his appearance pleasing. But more often, it was narrowed eyes and sneering looks. Rufus had found himself shying away from his family, however much he loved them, for as a man alone, he attracted no special interest – it was when he was among his pale, freckled relatives that the looks and whispers started.

When he had got the job, posted with the quaestor's staff to Africa Proconsularis, he had been excited. He would be miles away from his family, on another continent, and he could finally leave the rumours and the dirty looks behind. But his hopes had been dashed when Nasidienus boarded the boat. The man was a mean-spirited, jealous gossip, and more to the point, he had known the Curtius family for years and was well aware of Rufus' history.

Dinner on their first night in Adrumetum was no better.

Rufus could hear Nasidienus' grating, nasal voice drifting across the dining room, repeating the old rumours and accusations, pointing at his skin and hair. No one said anything to him directly, and Nasidienus' listeners mostly seemed to shuffle their feet and hands uncomfortably and try to change the subject, but for Rufus, it was inescapable. He lay in bed that night, wondering if he should quit this job all together, abandon his ambitions for a political career, and just go home to live quietly. He could marry some pretty but impoverished girl who would take him despite the scandal, and work on his history books. "After all," he told himself aloud, "it's not as if a political career means what it used to anyway. The Emperor and his staff do all the real work." But as he drifted off to sleep, he could hear his uncle's voice in his head, and he dreamed that the man's face appeared before him, telling him, as he had so many times, "You are a member of the Curtii! You belong to a great, historic family. You must do them proud, and serve your fatherland."

"But I'm not," he heard himself protesting weakly. "I'm not a real Curtius. Perhaps I should go off and be a gladiator, that's my heritage."

"You are a Curtius!" he heard his uncle say, dreaming himself back to his childhood hearth and seeing his uncle standing over him. "When you were nine days old, your father picked you up and carried you around the hearth-fire, just like so," and here, his uncle used to pick up one of the dogs to demonstrate, "and accepted you into his family. The Curtius family." And then his uncle leaned over and whispered in his ear, "And he could clearly see the colour of your skin when he did it."

Although it had been a somewhat restless night, Rufus found himself feeling distracted and fidgety all the next day, too. He was still unsure whether to stick it out, or give it all up and go home.

Mid-day came, and the quaestor announced that everyone would be retiring for a few hours. It was far too hot to work through the mid-day heat in this part of the world. Everyone else retired to their rooms, but Rufus was still unable to relax. Instead, he took himself off to the courtyard, to wander around the colonnade.

There was a small fountain and a garden of green trees and bushes in the open space at the centre of the villa. A little bronze statue of a drunk Hercules was eternally peeing fresh, clean water into a small pool. The ground was tiled in bright reds and blues, while the brickwork was painted in a mixture of blue and white. Birds sang and a light breeze blew off the sea as Rufus paced the colonnade. Even so close to the water, there was a dryness to the air that was very pleasant, and a sweet smell. Although not foolish enough to sit out in the sun, Rufus found that he liked the heat. It felt comforting, somehow, like the air was wrapping itself around him to protect him.

Rufus reached the section with that tiny view of the sea and started along it to continue his walk. But the air before him shimmered and suddenly he found his way was blocked. A woman, a huge woman, stood before him, the top of her head reaching the ceiling. Her skin was dark (far darker than his), and her lips full. She had a broad chest and a flat stomach, with slender legs and solid feet. Her black hair was twisted into dreadlocks, and she wore a rich robe in oranges, reds and yellows. She was the most beautiful woman Rufus had ever seen.

"I have heard of men seeing strange things in the desert," said Rufus, almost to himself, "but never in the courtyard!" He felt his forehead anxiously, thinking that perhaps he should have gone to lie down after all.

"I am no illusion of the desert, Quintus Curtius Rufus," said the woman, and her voice was rich and deep. "I am an African beacon-light, come to foretell your future."

"I don't understand," wavered Rufus.

The woman reached forward and took his chin in her huge hand, forcing him to look up at her. "You are home, Curtius Rufus," she said. "This is where you are meant to be. Stay here, work hard, and you will do well."

"Well?" stammered Rufus, wondering if the woman could be a bit more precise about this. As luck would have it, she could.

"Yes, well. You will serve three Emperors, and while so many others around you fall, you will stand tall. You will serve Rome across the Empire, all the way to Germania. You will be a general, and a consul. And then, one day, you will return here as proconsul to govern the whole province – and here, in your ancestral homeland, this is where you will die."

She let him go, the air shimmered once more, and she seemed to blow away on the sea breeze, leaving Rufus stunned and shaking. He sat down hard on the low garden wall and put his head in his hands. Her words about his "ancestral homeland" had shaken him more than he liked to admit. All his life, he had defended his mother against the rumours and the gossip, had told himself that he just tanned really easily. Now, the idea that his natural father might really be a gladiator – a slave! – was not a comfortable nor a happy one.

But he found he could pull himself together by focusing on the other part of her message. He would be a politician – a successful one! He would have a good career, would even become consul, something no member of the Curtius family had achieved for five hundred years. He would survive the Imperial court, would survive Imperial service, and die only once he had returned to this province as proconsul.

Rufus stood up with renewed energy, and despite the heat, found himself running down to the beach and hurling a stone defiantly into the sea as if to say, here I am – I'm staying here!

*****

Rome, 25 CE

"Pleased to meet you, young man. And what is it that you do?"

The Emperor did not look at all the way that Rufus had

imagined him. Everyone knew Tiberius was an unhappy and reluctant Emperor, so he had imagined him to be a grim and unpleasant man. Lurid stories were already starting to circulate about what the sixty-six-year-old got up to during his holidays to Campania, holidays which became longer and longer every year. Tiberius was flanked by Sejanus, officially Commander of the Praetorian Guard; unofficially, the man running the Empire. Sejanus' wide-set eyes and long nose stared down at Rufus, Nasidienus, and their fellow young, hopeful, aspiring politicians with disdain.

Tiberius, however, seemed quite pleasant in person. He looked tired, and a bit distracted, and an undercurrent of deep unhappiness flowed underneath his polite smile, threatening to burst forth if given a chance. He spent several minutes talking with each young man, and was at least skilled at pretending genuine interest in what they had to say.

"I was on the junior staff of the quaestor, sir," said Rufus. "I hope to stand for the quaestorship myself in the next few years." He heard Nasidienus snort.

"You're ambitious, then?" said the Emperor. "A political career is not all it's cracked up to be, you know."

Rufus looked down. "No Curtius has held a consulship in five hundred years," he said, "and I would like to break that trend. But I have other interests as well," he added defensively. "I have been working on a history of Alexander the Great."

"Really?" Tiberius seemed to perk up at this. "What is it that interests you about Alexander?"

"I suppose..." said Rufus hesitantly, having never really thought about it in depth. "I suppose it is simply that he did so much, in so short a time – and then died, having changed the world."

"Hmmm, yes," said Tiberius. "He was fortunate, he died young." The Emperor seemed to drift off into some private day dream until Sejanus pointedly cleared his throat over the old man's head. "Well, anyway," said Tiberius, shaking himself, "there is no reason to give up on your ambitions just yet, young man, if politics is really what you want."

"Excuse me sir," piped up Nasidienus from the other side of the room. The Emperor looked up sharply; the men on either side of Nasidienus shrank as far away from him as they could without getting up and walking away.

"Yes?

"Surely the writing of history would be far more suitable for someone like Rufus, sir?" sneered Nasidienus. "I know that your nephew Claudius enjoys it very much, and pursues it instead of a political career."

"My nephew is entirely unsuited to a political career," said Tiberius sharply. "He cannot speak properly, and he cannot stand or move properly, and without being able to stand up and give a convincing speech to move the hearts of the Senate and the people, a political career is impossible. But listening to Curtius Rufus here, I notice no such problems."

"But sir," persisted Nasidienus as the others moved even further away from him, "surely this man cannot represent the ancient family of the Curtii in the Senate? After all sir, you must have heard the rumours?"

A sudden hush fell across the room. Sejanus drew himself up even taller and narrowed his eyes at Nasidienus. Tiberius stood up slowly. He walked, first around Rufus, eyeing him up and down, watching him; Rufus stood completely still and kept his eyes ahead, willing himself not to break. Then Tiberius walked over to Nasidienus, and walked around him too. Once, twice. Then he motioned to Sejanus, who motioned to a guard, who came over and walked Nasidienus out of the room.

"Let all here understand this clearly," he said. "I regard Curtius Rufus as his own father. And that is all anyone should have to say on the matter."

Rufus sighed out his relief as the Emperor motioned for him to move aside and make way for the next man. He could see the corners of Sejanus' mouth turning up, just a little, into a smile. The other young men in the room nodded silently.

*****

Carthage, 58 CE

Curtius Rufus stood once more near the prow of a ship as it approached the harbour at Carthage. He had not returned to Africa Proconsularis since he had left with Nasidienus and the quaestor and all the other junior staff, more than thirty years ago. He suppressed a tiny, mean-spirited smile at the memory of Nasidienus. The man had faded into obscurity after their meeting with Tiberius, and Rufus had not seen or even thought of him in years.

Tiberius had retired not long after their meeting, but Rufus had never forgotten his kindness – and nor, he suspected, had anyone else, at least anyone still alive who remembered that meeting. Sejanus had been given the position of consul, the highest position in Rome besides Emperor, but that same year had been accused of treason and executed. Trials for treason became as common as a weekly fruit market, and many of the other young men Rufus had grown up with were caught up in the political turmoil and killed. Then even more of them were executed under Tiberius' successor Gaius Caligula, for a variety of reasons, some more sane and logical than others.

Rufus had survived, though, disappearing to bury himself in his history of Alexander whenever things seemed to be getting too heated. Throughout it all, he had remembered the words of the African spirit – that he would become consul, and that eventually he would return to Africa. If he were executed for treason, or for criticising one of Caligula's theatrical shows (as others had been), he would never return to Africa. So he kept his head down and wrote his book, trusting that if he did so, things would work out, somehow.

And then, the miracle happened – Tiberius' lame, stammering nephew Claudius the historian became Claudius the Emperor. This new Emperor had thoroughly approved of Rufus' history-writing and suddenly his career took off as it never had before. He was made consul – the first Curtius in five hundred years! Claudius even awarded him the honour of Triumphal insignia for his work on a silver mine in Germania, even though it had not turned out to be as profitable as he had hoped.

And now he was to govern the whole province of Africa as proconsul. The night before he left Rome for the last time, he had gone to see the Emperor to thank him for everything he had done.

"D-don't m-mention it," Claudius assured him. "We survivors m-must st-stick together."

"You were never... worried about promoting me?" asked Rufus. It was the closest he had come to mentioning the rumours and gossip for years.

Claudius laughed. "P-promoting you?" he said. "Never! You should hear the r-rumours ab-out me!"

The ship docked. Rufus smiled at the coin of Claudius in his hand and stepped off onto the shores of Africa. Even though the air smelled of the salt of the sea, he could taste the desert in it as well, just on the edge of his senses. It was once again a spring day, and it was warm, verging on hot. Rufus hopped down onto the beach, walking away from the men unloading all his supplies, and strolled along the shore for a few minutes.

The air in front of him shimmered and went hazy. The sand swirled, spinning up into a whirlwind of stone and grit and sea salt, and then – there she was. The enormous woman with her dark skin and tight dreadlocks, looking over him in the midday sunshine, and smiling.

"Welcome back, Curtius Rufus," she said warmly.

"I did it!" he told her happily. "I served three Emperors, I survived when everyone else around me was dying, I went to Germania and won a Triumph," – suddenly he stopped as he remembered the last part of the prophecy. "Have you brought me back here to die?" he asked.

She laughed. "I have not brought you anywhere, you have made your way back here on your own merits, and maybe a little bit of luck!" she told him. "But yes – you will die here, and you can be laid to rest here, at home." And with that, in another swirl of sand and shimmer of mist, she was gone.

Rufus bent over double in a sudden pain that disappeared as abruptly as it had come, and returned, shaken, to his companions. That evening, he wrote to Claudius.

"Sir, I write once again to thank you for your patronage. I am to die soon – although my men and my physician insist there is nothing really wrong, the spirit that has watched over me throughout my career has reminded me that it is soon to end. I wish to be buried here in Africa, near the amphitheatre in Thysdrus, but please know that I have left all my lands in Rome to you in my will. Do not mourn for me. I am home."

FINIS

A TORTURED SOUL

Inspired by Suetonius, *Caligula*, 59

A peacock screeches. Have you ever heard a peacock screech? It's a sound that goes right through your body, telling your every nerve that something is desperately wrong.

Shouts and a general clamour from the next hill. More screams, human this time. Is that blood running down the gutter from the imperial palace?

A body lies in a lake of fresh blood in a covered corridor that leads from the outside into the Emperor's house. Stabbed more than thirty times in every part of the body, even the most private, and his jawbone split. His body slaves lift him and take him to his wife, but the assassins are close behind, and wife and infant daughter quickly follow him to the afterlife. The slaves retreat, terrified.

This is the scene that greets Herod Agrippa when he finally tracks down his friend; Gaius Caligula, Emperor, madman, fool, and god.
 "We should get out of here, Sire," says Blastus, clutching at the king's sleeve in his panic.
 "No," says Herod, shaking him off. "Not yet. You said Caesonia is dead?"

"And the baby," confirms Blastus.

"And no one knows where his uncle Claudius is?"

"No, Sire," says Blastus. "No one has seen him."

"Then all his heirs are gone, or trapped miles away in exile," says Herod.

"Because he exiled them," mutters Blastus, but he does so under his breath. When a man's close friend is lying dead at his feet in a pool of blood, it is not the time to start criticising his family relationships. When the survivor is a king, it is best not to criticise his friends at all.

"According to their custom, if there are no heirs, then anyone who owed money to the deceased and hadn't paid it is responsible for seeing to their proper burial and all the required rituals."

"Sire, you aren't going to carry out some pagan ritual and worship the man, are you?" says Blastus nervously. The Romans had some strange rituals around their dead. They were simultaneously afraid of them, and yet treated them like minor gods requiring offerings and (rather sombre) festivals. The *Manes*, they called them – the Shades. And Caligula was no ordinary Roman. Blastus has seen this Emperor demand worship in his own city, and even worse, demand that his statue be placed in the Temple in Jerusalem. He suspects nothing can really surprise him any more, not even a Jewish king carrying out a Roman pagan death ritual.

But Herod is not impressed. "Of course not!" he snaps, shoving Blastus to one side and kneeling down by his friend in the blood. "But they believe to be improperly buried is a terrible fate, that the ghost of a person not buried properly haunts the Earth in torment and cannot rest. We can cremate him and bury him at least. Beyond that, his soul will have to fend for itself. Go and find some slaves and get them back here – drag them by the hair if you have to!"

Blastus scurries off to look for the household slaves. Not far away, Herod can hear Gaius' German bodyguard running riot around the palace, furious at the death of their master and ready to blame anyone but themselves for what was clearly a spectacular failure on their part. On his way over here, Herod saw them killing senators almost at random – some he was fairly sure had been involved in the assassination, others he was almost certain had not.

"Oh, my friend," Herod sighs, sinking down by the body. "How did it come to this? You, the handsome darling of Rome for six months, despite the falling sickness." And then he stops talking, for it is not proper to speak ill of the dead. He knows the man was troubled. He remembers the strange illness that nearly killed him a few months into his reign, the slow recovery. He remembers the headaches, the sleepless nights, and the tormented thoughts that raged in Gaius' brain. He remembers a letter he received when Gaius had gone to the coast with the army on manoeuvres, complaining that the Ocean itself was talking to him, teasing him, threatening him. He remembers the paranoia, the recklessness, and the cruel treatment of even the man's sisters, cousins, uncle. Herod is not unaware of Gaius' flaws.

And yet he loves him, even now, lying in that lake of blood, his body mangled and abused. He loves the memory of nights out and drinking parties and playing dice into the small hours of the morning in their younger days. Even in the bad years when it all started to go sour and Gaius fell more and more prey to his own troubled soul, he loves the passion, he even loves the recklessness a little bit. Love is love, perhaps. And so Herod gently lifts the body, takes it to the nearest room, and lays it on a couch. He tears off a piece of curtain to cover the face, and he takes off the soldiers' sandals that gave Gaius his nickname when he was two years old – Little Boot, Caligula.

Blastus returns, bringing a gaggle of reluctant slaves with him. Hastily, they wrap the body up in a sheet and throw it onto a litter, which they carry as quickly as possible across the hill to the Lamian gardens, the pine trees standing sentinel among the bare January pots and flowerbeds. Others carry wood and kindling for the pyre. The winter sun peeks through the haze as they build the pyre, light it, step back.

"Now what?" asks Blastus, adding "Sire" before he forgets.

"We stand vigil," says Herod.

"Like sitting shiva?" asks Blastus.

"Yes, I suppose so," says Herod. "We stand and watch until the body is completely burned. Only when the body is fully burned and the remaining ash and bones buried can the spirit rest." He pauses. "Though half a burning will ensure the body cannot be desecrated by his enemies," he adds, glancing towards the Palatine Hill, where more noises and shouts can be heard.

A slave brings Herod a folding chair and he wraps his blood-stained robes around him and sits down. Blastus, with a nod of permission, kneels on the ground beside him and they watch the pale sun slip towards the skyline.

More noise, more shouting. A man appears, breathing heavily from unaccustomed running. It is Claudius' slave, Narcissus.

"Sire! King Herod!" Narcissus gasps, choking on the ash and spitting out bits of ex-Emperor as he rushes to find them. "They told me you were here!"

"Who told you?" asks Herod, just the tiniest edge of panic in his voice. "What is it?"

"The Emperor's slaves," says Narcissus in answer to the first question. "Sire, my master needs you!"

"Claudius is alive?!" cries Herod, jumping up from his seat.

"A soldier found him where he was hiding in the palace – they dragged him out and declared him Emperor – they have taken him to their camp – the senate has met and they are talking about bringing back the Republic – Sire, we do not know what to do." Narcissus hunches over, wheezing, tears in his eyes.

"What do you mean you do not know what to do?" cries Herod. "He must claim the throne! The Senate will not allow him to live if they restore the Republic. He must act if he wishes to last the night!"

"Well come and tell him that, for Jove's sake!" cries

Narcissus, forgetting for a moment that he is a slave talking to a king. "He is in a blind panic and talking about running away!"

"There is nowhere to run to," says Herod. "You Romans have taken over the whole world – all the inhabitable parts of it anyway." He closes his eyes briefly, takes a deep breath. "We will come straight away." He glances towards the pyre as the small sun disappears behind the hill, and then looks to the huddle of Gaius' slaves standing in its flickering light. "See that he cannot be recognised, then take him off the pyre and bury him here," Herod commands, "and then come to the Camp to look after your new master. Blastus, see to it that they do it." And with one last glance, he strides away down the hill towards the camp, Narcissus scurrying breathlessly at his heels. Blastus turns a grumpy face towards the slaves and snaps at them to get on with it, pulling his cloak around him and standing uncomfortably close to the pyre to fight off the January cold.

*****

A warm spring breeze blows through the gardens. It is evening, and the peacocks are resting in the treetops. From around the brightly coloured marble pillars of the bathhouse, two immaculately dressed women head a small, solemn train of slaves and freedwomen. A few steps behind these courtly ladies, the watchmen of the gardens are guiding them past caged tigers, statues of Bacchus and Venus and Priapus, and elaborate frescos, to a small and apparently unassuming flowerbed.

"It is here, my ladies," says the First Watchman, gesturing towards this patch of earth. It has obviously been worked over relatively recently, but zinnia flowers in red, yellow, and purple are already standing proud across a distinct hump in the ground. "This is where the late Emperor is buried. Are you wishing to say prayers to the *Manes*, Mistress Agrippina, Mistress Livilla?"

Livilla nods but Agrippina has other ideas. "Far more than that," she says. "We intend to have him excavated, properly cremated, and interred in the Mausoleum of our great-grandfather Augustus with the proper ceremonies."

There is a sharp intake of breath from Livilla, who sees in her mind's eye the anger of the assassins and the fragility of their uncle Claudius's new regime. She hears almost as if they were being spoken out loud the ugly rumours about her and her sister's relationship with their late brother, and feels sure that this act of sisterly devotion will be mis-interpreted by the gossips eager to spread salacious rumours of incest and orgies and all kinds of sexual deviance.

But Agrippina is confident. She see the doubt written on her sister's face, and puts a consoling arm around her. "We are Antigone," she says, squeezing Livilla's shoulder. "Oedipus' daughter knew that family is what matters, more than anything else. She knew she had to make sure her traitorous brother was properly buried. We too will defy the laws of man to obey the laws of the gods and bury our foolish, mistaken brother in the proper way."

"Antigone ended up dead, if I remember the play correctly," says Livilla, shaking off her sister's arm and refraining from suggesting that comparing themselves to a mythological character most famously born of incest is probably not a good idea if they want to convince the general public of their innocence. But as she looks up she sees to her surprise that the watchmen have expressions of delight on both their faces.

"Truly, mistress?" asks the Second Watchman eagerly. "You are going to give him a full and proper burial rite?"

"That pleases you, watchman?" says Agrippina, making an I-told-you-so face at her sister. "You think this act of piety is worth doing?"

"It's not that Mistress," says the Second Watchman, as the First tries to hush him. "It's more that in doing so you will put his soul to rest."

"What are you talking about?" asks Livilla, while Agrippina

raises a sceptical eyebrow.

"Every night, we see it," says the Second Watchman, ignoring the First grabbing at his arm, trying to make him stop talking. "For hours and hours, he wanders the gardens in the dark, complaining of a headache, or crying out that the Ocean is plotting against him. Blood pours from his wounds in an endless flood and he cries out, 'You can't kill me, I'm a god!'"

"Hush, man!" snaps the First Watchmen, kicking the Second viciously in the leg. "My ladies, I am so sorry. Please ignore this superstitious old woman here."

"Is he telling the truth?" Livilla asks him. "Please speak freely. Have you seen and heard this thing as well?"

The First Watchman shifts uncomfortably. He looks from the face of one royal lady to the other, trying to work out what they want to hear, what will keep him alive and in a job. Agrippina is implacable, her expression gives away nothing. Livilla is pleading. She almost seems to want to hear stories of her brother's restless spirit. In the end, he decides to go with the truth, and let Fate decide what to do with him.

"I have seen and heard things, yes, my lady," he says. "It is as my companion says. I have seen a bloodied figure restlessly pacing these grounds throughout the night; I have heard cries and screams and low moans."

"That settles it," says Agrippina firmly. "He must be properly buried in our family Mausoleum without delay. We will have a full family funeral – Uncle Claudius does not have to come, that might look bad, but my son Nero and his cousins should be there."

"Yes," says Livilla with a sigh. An image of an actor playing Antigone flashes across her vision and she suddenly has a premonition; she will not long survive this task. She has always thought that Agrippina would survive Deucalion's Flood, though if the past few years of watching a sister, three brothers, a cousin and a brother-in-law fall one by one to the curse of imperial paranoia have taught her anything, it is that no one is safe. She suspects Agrippina has a least a few more years though; the woman could survive by sheer determination alone. Perhaps, if she helps with this, her sister will do her the same favour, and her soul will be spared from wandering the earth with their brother.

The sun disappears beneath the horizon and they turn to go. As they walk out of the gardens, both women become aware of a restless stirring behind them. Livilla glances towards the watchmen. They are both staring straight ahead, towards the gates, their heads not turning, their eyes fixed on the way out. She hears a moaning sound, the low groaning of a man in pain. Then it is joined by a sound like feet in soldiers' sandals, hobbling down the path behind them. She can hear the clink of the fastenings with each step, and the softer sound of the hobnailed boots crunching along the gravelled path. No one says anything, but even Agrippina picks up the pace.

At the gate, they have to wait a moment while the slaves open it, and the watchmen settle themselves into their positions. The moaning gets louder and and the hobnailed footsteps seem to be getting closer and closer. Agrippina is tight-lipped, her mouth pursed. Livilla is wide-eyed and shaking. Both dive through the gate as quickly as possible in a somewhat unladylike fashion.

"We will send the slaves to exhume him tomorrow," says Agrippina to a silent nod from Livilla, as a low moan carries the words, "My head, my head….." across to them on the night wind.

*****

A hot, dry July night, years later, and Rome is burning. The baking heat of summer in the city has been turned into a furnace by a fire that has raged for five days and five nights so far. The flames have been licking the edge of the imperial land on the Palatine Hill since they broke out, but now they are engulfing it.

The watchmen in the old Emperor's house are in a state of panic. Emperor Nero has finally stopped singing long enough to come to the city to oversee the fire-fighting. If someone finds out they abandoned their posts, they will not see another night. The man has murdered his own mother, step-brother, wife, and aunt; he will have no mercy for a few frightened watchmen.

On the other hand, there seems little point saving oneself from execution by dying in an inferno. The last two watchmen left find each other in a small room with a few couches in it; they look at each other; they nod.

But it is too late. There is no way out. All the exits are blocked by fire and smoke, and the pool in the atrium is boiling.

Only one exit has not yet been consumed by the flames – the covered corridor. It will lead them out of the house, but to enter into a covered area full of smoke seems like setting foot on a path straight to Hades. And there is something else – for these men have worked here for a long time, and they know what awaits them in that corridor…

Having no other choice, the two watchmen dive forward into the gloom together.

Out of the smoke, a dark shadow rises before their soot-covered faces. A man, or something that used to be a man, the mere suggestion of a face in the darkness, the bones gleaming through the echo of his skin. He is bleeding from every part of his body, even the most private. He is both terrifying and sadly pathetic, this creature. He moans and groans and reaches out his battered arms towards them. "You can't kill me, I'm a god!" the monster screams, then clutches his bloody head and calls out in a low voice, "My head, my head…"

The watchmen have seen this thing before. Before, always, they have fled in terror, finding some other room to watch, some other gate to guard. But now, there is nowhere to go but back into the fire.

The two men grip each other's hands silently in the smoke, choking on the ash of the palace's funeral pyre. They take a breath – small, shallow, just enough to propel them out of there – and together they run right through the image of the dead Emperor. For a moment, their clothes gleam red with phantom blood and the shadows of broken arms reach out to grab at them and pull them back. But it is insubstantial, this spectre, and it cannot stop them. They run and they run, until they burst out of the corridor and into the open air.

For just a moment, they turn around to look back at the palace. They made it just in time – the flames have engulfed the whole building now, and the walls are crumbling before their eyes.

Just in front of the house, at the end of the corridor, they see the bloodied figure raise up its arms to the heavens, and then it seems to be consumed by the flames. As the corridor itself falls into a smouldering ruin, the figure disappears, as if eaten up by the inferno. Then, for a moment, there is a feeling of absolute peace. It is as if a hanging threat, the despair of a soul troubled throughout life and death, has been lifted. There is a moment of calm.

The flames rise higher and the watchmen turn and flee. Whatever new evils may rise in its place, this one at least will not return.

FINIS

DIES IRAE

Inspired by Suetonius, *Nero*, 34

There was another fire in our neighbourhood last week. An apartment building just across the street from ours burned down. I thought that we'd had it, that surely the sparks would set ours alight as well, but we were saved by a well-timed thunderstorm, thank Jupiter. I swear, one of these days, the whole Subura is going to go up.

I'll never get another set of rooms as good as this if I have to move. Right on the ground floor – no stairs! – with the shop-front facing out into the street, it's perfect. I've got a huge sign up right next to the front door; NAUSICAA, SPECIALIST DREAM INTERPRETER. Usually, if the weather is good, I put out a little wooden stand with some copies of my book in beautiful saffron-stained parchment covers (with a male pen name on display, which helps the sales) – but of course, it caught an unlucky spark from the bloody fire last week and the whole lot went up in flames. So now I'm out several very expensive copies, and struggling to sell the simple plain copies I keep tucked away in the back of the shop.

I thought my luck was changing when he walked in. He was trying to disguise how rich he was, I could see that straight away. Probably a good idea, in this part of Rome, though I have to say, I've seen better disguises. He had put on a big, brown hooded cloak, the hood pulled across his face, over his gleaming white toga, which was poking out around his ankles. He was surrounded by a group of six burly men who were dressed in plain tunics to look like slaves, but were carrying shinier short swords than I have ever seen a slave armed with. They walked tall, shoulders back, stepping in unison; like soldiers.

Their boss was a senator in disguise, I was sure of it. That meant he had money. Lots of money. Lots of money I badly needed.

"Welcome, welcome!" I said, putting on my friendliest face. "What brings you here today?"

"You're the dream interpreter?" The voice was not what I expected. I was prepared for gravitas, for a gravelly old voice that had seen too many years, or maybe for a weaselly ancient whine. But this man's voice was neither. It was a young voice, but with the aggression and confidence of someone much older. It was a voice that did not just *expect* everyone it addressed to obey it – it *knew* that everyone it spoke to *would* obey it.

"That's right, the dream interpreter, that's me!" I said, too brightly. "How can I help you today?"

"You do... cures as well?" the imperious voice asked. "Treatments?" As his mouth moved, I caught sight of a weedy bit of neck-beard moving around on a double chin.

"I do indeed," I said. I moved towards the back of the shop, intending to price up some bags of frankincense for him (at inflated senatorial prices, I'm no fool). If I'm honest, I also just wanted to stand a bit further away from him. He was giving me the creeps.

"I have been told you are very good," he said. "That is why we have made our way out here." He glanced outside the door towards the Subura and wrinkled up his nose. "I need a cure for some troubling dreams I have been having."

"Certainly," I said, gesturing to the comfortable recliner I keep in the shop for clients to relax on while they tell me about their problems. "Tell me your dreams."

He bristled, and I noticed all the bodyguards around him standing up a little taller.

"My dreams are private," the young man said.

I steeled myself and, lightning fast, made a choice. Should I go along with him, offer him something to make him feel better and make it seem like I had helped, but potentially watch my whole business fall apart when word got out that I was a fraud who didn't even bother finding out what a dream was before prescribing a cure for it? Or should I stand my ground and insist on doing my job properly, even if the client was rich and famous?

If I had known then what I know now, I think I would have made a different decision.

"I'm afraid I can't help you unless you tell me something about your dreams," I said.

With a gesture of his head, my visitor dismissed all his bodyguards out into the street. He threw back his hood dramatically and drew himself up, obviously expecting me to recognise him instantly. I didn't, but his full face and fuzzy, thin strip of a beard did look vaguely familiar in a way that tugged at the back of my mind.

He sighed and threw himself onto the recliner, lolling his head back dramatically.

"I can't sleep!" he proclaimed, as if to the very back of the audience at the theatre.

"Indeed," I said, twisting my fingers together to stop myself shouting at him to just blurt it out already.

'Every night," he said, lying back and staring at the ceiling, "as I lie down in bed, I hear a weird swooshing sound, and the hissing of snakes. A wind comes from nowhere and blows open the door of my bedroom. I look towards it, and there's a woman standing there, or a monster in the shape of a woman. She has sharp, pointed wings, and there are snakes coiling around her all over her body – in her hair, around her arms, and circling around her waist like a belt. She holds a fiery torch in one hand, and in the other is a whip that she cracks across the floor of the room, grazing my feet as I sit up on the bed. She's in the shadows but I can see her face by the light of the torch and I can see that she is angry – furious. Her teeth are bared and she's snarling at me. Then she moves forward, right into the light, and suddenly I realise it's my mother."

"Fascinating," I say, to fill time. "Can you tell me about your mother? What is she like?"

"She's dead," he said shortly. I waited, but it seemed nothing else was forthcoming.

I pulled out a copy of my book from the back of the shop and opened up the scroll to the section on dreams of one's mother.

"Did you have intercourse with your mother in the dream?" I asked.

"In the dream?" he said. "No."

I let the implication of the question slide and carried on. "Right, well we'll skip past that section then," I said, skimming quite far down the book. "As you can see here, dreaming of one's mother being angry with oneself foretells a dishonourable way of life. Are you thinking of doing something dishonourable?"

"This interview is at an end," the man said, standing up. "Your reputation is clearly undeserved. You cannot even remember the contents of the book you claim to have written."

"No, no!" I cried in protest. "I was just showing you where you could look up the information, if you were to take a copy home with you today. I will prescribe something for your dreams. I would strongly recommend you burn frankincense and sacrifice a lamb before an altar of Asclepius -" but I was cut off.

"You are a charlatan," he said, "and you will be punished accordingly."

"I need more information!" I cried to his retreating back as he headed towards the door. "I can tell you that your mother's appearance is similar to that of the Furies, the goddesses of vengeance, and that the dream seems focused around anger in some way. But without more information about her and about your relationship, I can give only the most basic recommendations."

The man stopped and snatched the scroll from my hands, looking over it.

"You have dream interpretations for *slaves* in here!" he said in astonishment.

"Slaves have dreams too," I said.

He stared at me in the fading light, and narrowed his eyes. "You are strange, and not nearly frightened enough," he said, which struck me as a very odd thing to say. "I will give you one more chance. I have hired a group of Magi to perform a ritual tomorrow that they promise will get to the bottom of these infernal dreams. If it doesn't, I will have their heads," he chortled to himself. "You will attend. We will meet at the Mausoleum of my divine forefather Augustus, at twilight. You will learn whatever you need to learn from the ritual, and you will make a recommendation. And we will see."

He swept out of the shop, leaving me quivering in my sandals. As he turned around, I realised where I recognised him from. I pulled out a coin from my purse and stared at the plump, bearded face of the Emperor Nero.

*****

I thought about fleeing for my life that night, but with no money and no family to run to, I did not know where to go. So the following evening, I made my way to the Mausoleum of Augustus.

I had passed by the Mausoleum many times, the great round tomb overlooking the Campus Martius. In the daytime, its white walls shine brightly in the sunlight, and the shade of the tall cypresses planted on its upper terrace barely reaches the ground. If you look up and squint, you can just about make out the colossal statue of the late, now Divine, Emperor Augustus perched on the top. At night, though, it is a dark shadow looming over the buildings around it, while the pink granite obelisks at the entrance stand guard.

There I was met by Nero's bodyguards, now out of their simple disguises and smartly dressed in their uniforms, and a small group of nervy Persian priests, the Magi.

There were three of them, and they had gone all out with their outfits; they were dressed in the full garb of the ancient Persian magicians, wearing soft red Phrygian caps and long robes over brightly patterned trousers, with oiled beards – I have to confess, they smelled really rather lovely.

"Follow us," announced one of the guards.

"This ritual should be performed at the tomb of the deceased," one of the Magi said tentatively.

At that, the Emperor revealed himself, stepping out of the doorway. In his wake was a small slave boy carrying a big wooden box, an ugly brand stamped across his forehead.

"There will be no need to travel to my mother's tomb," Nero declared. I saw his guards exchange glances and wondered what sort of tomb, or attempt at one, he had put his mother in. No wonder her spirit was haunting him if she was not even buried properly. "This is the mausoleum of my family, of the Divine Augustus and his successors. You will be perfectly able to perform your ritual here."

There was no point in trying to argue. The gloomy priests and I shuffled through the open door one by one, into the darkness of the tomb.

We followed the guards, carrying torches, down a corridor through the mass of earth and concrete that made up most of the huge structure, to the circular burial chamber at its centre. The walls rose high around us as we walked around the golden funerary urns of the Imperial family, the torchlight showing us surprisingly small inscriptions in honour of each one. The Emperor led the way to the spot he had chosen, in front of the urn of the Divine Augustus himself. The guards stepped back and stood against the walls, holding their torches high. The Magi and I gathered in a small semi-circle in the flickering light, facing the Emperor, who stood in front of his godly ancestor's urn and stared out at us.

One of the Magi cleared his throat and said nervously,

"Did you bring the offerings we need, my lord?"

Nero flicked a finger to the slave boy, who opened up the box he was carrying and produced some small offerings. Nero took a series of small jars in turn, naming each as he poured out libations onto the smooth floor with a splash.

"Milk from an un-mated cow," he said, pouring out the first, and then, "clear honey, blessed water from a virgin spring, and unmixed wine." After the libations came some more solid offerings, which he placed carefully at the foot of the plinth that held Augustus' urn. "The fruit of the olive tree, an immortal plant, and a garland of flowers, the children of the earth."

"It is good," said one of the Magi. "We will make the incantation, and summon the spirit back to earth."

It was only at that moment that I realised what kind of ritual they were performing. My stomach plummeted to my feet and I stepped back a little – but that meant stepping out of the circle of torchlight and into the blackness of the mausoleum, so I stepped forward again and pulled my arms tightly across my chest, shivering.

"Mithra, Rashnu, Soroush, and the lords of the underworld!" intoned the first of the priests. "Send to us here, on the earth above, the Shade of the late Empress, Agrippina the Younger!"

"Lords of the underworld, send her Shade back to this earth above! Send us our beloved mother, Agrippina the Younger!" declared the second.

"Be her guide, oh lords of the underworld!" chanted the third. "Send the Shade of Agrippina the Younger from below the earth to her old place here up above."

For a moment, nothing happened. But then, the ground began to rumble beneath our feet, and the solid earth walls trembled. The torches flickered and an eerie glow rose up the sides of the old Emperor's golden urn from the bottom to the top.

We all stepped back as the solid floor started to ripple and swirl like water. Out of the very earth rose the figure of a woman, tall and straight as a statue, but with hair that had once been neatly styled half torn out and unkempt, wearing a blue stola that was covered in blood. Her petite facial features were twisted into a snarl and her hands were raised, fingers spread like claws, ready to attack.

The instant he saw her, Nero fell to his face on the floor. "Forgive me, mother!" he cried, and he tried to clasp her knees in supplication. But there was no substance to her body, and his arms passed right through her legs, and he fell to the floor on his face once more.

"Do you know what I said to that oaf you sent to me with his sword drawn?" the phantom snarled, in a voice like sawdust in a sandstorm. She leaned down over her son's prostrate form, almost but not quite touching him. The rest of us shrank back as far as we dared, so the torchlight shifted and left the pair of them in sweeping shadows, among the ashes of their family.

Nero shook his head, and the Shade raised herself up a little, seemingly changing the subject.

"The first time you tried to kill me," she said, almost conversationally, "I thought it was a mistake. I realised what had happened, took the antidote, and assumed that Octavia was your intended target. The second time, I thought you were getting sloppy. By the third time, I could no longer deny the truth." The shadow of a hand stroked the quivering Emperor's back, as he buried his face in his hands on the floor and would not look at her.

"You were a nightmare from the moment I realised I was pregnant, you know," rasped the phantom, apparently switching subjects again. "I puked my guts out for seven months solid, did I ever tell you? I could barely eat, sleep, or walk. I put my whole life on hold, trying to protect and nurture yours, you little ingrate. It took three days for you to be born, in the middle of winter, when the nights are long and the days are grey. The midwives were despairing of both of us when you finally arrived, and I swore I would never let your father touch me again. I stuck to that, too, and I made sure your great-uncle Claudius could never put me through that again either – not that there would have been any life left in his old seed by that time, anyway."

I felt the priest next to me shudder, whether in horror or revulsion, I was not sure.

"So you can imagine how I felt, puking out poison and antidote together, when I realised you were trying to kill me again," the thing that had been Agrippina continued. "I hired a new food taster, I stopped taking food or drink that had been anywhere near you or your dirty freedmen. And then, there was the boat."

I glanced up towards the grey-blue figure, interested despite myself. Like everyone else in Rome, I had heard the rumours.

"However did you persuade some idiot to captain a collapsible ship?" the ghost inquired, and Nero moaned low from his position on the floor. "And what made you think I couldn't swim?" She leaned down and hissed in his ear, but it was loud enough still to be heard. "What made you think," she said, her tongue whipping out, snake-like, "that I would not push my friend down and use her as a raft to save myself? Acceronia sends greetings, by the way. She does not hold it against me – she would have done the same herself."

The figure stood tall once more and repeated its first question. "Do you know what I said to the brute who killed me?" Nero raised his head to look up at her. "I told him to stab me right here," she poked herself hard in her abdomen, ripping her blue dress, "to take out my wretched womb first, from whence all the malice and bile and poison that is you came!"

"Forgive me," repeated Nero in a barely-audible whisper.

"Never!" exclaimed the ghost, and it spun itself around in a tempest of shadows, and disappeared.

"Dismissed," said Nero to us, quietly, from the floor. Then, when we did not move, he sat up and screamed, "DISMISSED!" at the top of his voice. The three Magi fled blindly down the pitch dark corridor and out of the mausoleum.

I hesitated. I did not think Nero would be inclined to let anyone who had witnessed his humiliation live, and I had nowhere to run to, nor could I run fast enough to outpace Imperial assassins if I did. But he just might allow someone who had helped him their life, if they were lucky.

I cleared my throat. "My lord," I mumbled. "My lord, I think I can help."

Nero slowly stood and brushed off his toga. He steadied himself against the Divine Augustus' plinth.

"Speak," he said.

I took a deep breath. I had to be all in, or nothing.

"My lord, is it true that your mother killed your adoptive father, the Divine Claudius, with a poisoned mushroom?"

Nero was surprised enough by the question to actually answer it for once.

"It is true," he said.

"Then here is my cure," I said. "There is a trilogy of Greek plays that tell of a family tragedy. The mother, Clytemnestra, murders the father, Agamemnon, in revenge for his sacrifice of their older daughter. Her son, Orestes, is forced to avenge his father by committing matricide and murdering her."

"Do you think I don't know the *Oresteia*, peasant?" exclaimed the Emperor, his voice rising again.

"Of course, of course!" I held out my hands in supplication. "My point is, Orestes is chased by the Furies for committing the crime of matricide – as you have been yourself, your mother appearing in the form of a Fury in your dreams, venting her rage upon you."

Nero appeared to think about this. "The flaming torch, the coiling snakes... yes, yes! How did I not see it before?" For the first time in our short acquaintance, he looked impressed. "Carry on," he said.

"Orestes was tried by the gods at the court of Athens and pardoned, because the mother provides only the earth for a man to grow, it is the father who creates the seed – and so the father outranks and outweighs the mother in importance." I trusted that Nero was not in a frame of mind to pick holes in this argument, and point out that the late Emperor Claudius was his adoptive father, not his biological parent. "To lay to rest the Shade of your mother and prevent her from hounding you, you must put on a production of the *Oresteia* and play the part of Orestes yourself. You will act out the trial before the whole of the people of Rome, and the gods themselves will pardon you for the righteous vengeance you exacted on your mother, to pay for the murder of your father, and your nights will finally be at peace."

Nero's face lit up. He sprang away from the plinth and snatched a torch from one of his bodyguards, spinning around in glee and crying,

"Yes! Yes, you smart little dream-woman! That is it!"

I had gambled, and guessed correctly that any solution that allowed him to indulge his love of theatre would be well received.

Nero scampered away down the corridor, already shouting instructions for preparations to be made for the production to the slave boy who hurried behind him, hauling the heavy wooden box full of half empty jars. The guards ran after him, and I hurried behind their retreating torchlight, not wishing to be left alone in the dark in that hole full of dead emperors. But as I went, I gave the urn of the Divine Augustus a quick kiss, and offered up a prayer that this play would heal the Emperor's mind enough that he would be able to sleep, and I would keep my life.

*****

The Emperor was so pleased with my advice, that I was given special permission to sit with the men for the performance, which was to be in the great Theatre of Pompey, a stone's throw from where Nero's illustrious forebear Julius Caesar had breathed his last. And so I found myself seated among Nero's freedmen, a disparate group of terrified survivors, odious sycophants, and men who had long ago buried their memories in wine. All three plays were performed in one day, with fairly long breaks in between each for food and, of course, drink.

Nero appeared in both the second and third plays, *The Libation Bearers* and *Eumenides*, or *The Furies*, as we called it. He wore a bizarre theatrical mask that seemed to have been modelled after his own features – it even included his distinctive neck-beard around the rim. The idea of allowing oneself to disappear into a character and be consumed by it was clearly entirely foreign to him. Nero's sole interest in the theatre – and in life – was in displaying his own imagined skills and virtues to the world.

His actual performance was rather over the top, but at least you could not call it boring. The classical Greek custom of abstaining from showing any violence on the stage, and allowing the Chorus to paint a picture of the bloodshed that lay behind the story with their song, did not appeal to the Emperor. When the moment came for him, as Orestes, to murder his mother Clytemnestra, he attacked the actor playing Clytemnestra on stage, in full view of everyone, with what I can only hope were stage tricks and false blood. When the time came for Orestes to start seeing the Furies chasing him in his mind, not only were there pantomime actors on stage playing the part of the Furies, but the Emperor over-pronounced every line and waved his arms around dramatically so much that I would never have believed he had experienced such visions in reality if I had not seen it with my own eyes.

When his character was exonerated at the end of the third play, and given the support of the gods Apollo and Minerva, Nero whipped off his theatrical mask all together to allow us all to see his grin of triumph. He put it on again to leave the stage, at which point I realised that the mask worn by the actor playing Apollo had been modelled after the features of the Divine Augustus, just to really drive the point home.

As soon as the performance was finished, I was summoned to the Emperor's dressing-room, to find him jubilant and thoroughly pleased with how everything had gone.

"Of course, I prefer the Trojan War cycle myself," he said, as he clapped me on the back and thanked me for my help. "Or *The Madness of Hercules*. But this – what an experience! What a cure! I could feel the forgiveness of the gods bestowed upon me as I sat on that stage, I could feel it I tell you! I shall sleep well tonight."

"I am glad to hear it, my lord," I said. I did not intend to wait and find out if my plan had worked, if his mind would now forgive its own crimes, heal itself, and allow him to rest. While the Emperor was planning his grand performance, I had written a letter to a distant cousin I had long ago lost touch with, who had married a barbarian merchant and moved to some wet, windswept island called Britain, which Rome had only recently conquered, in the far north. I was to ride out to Ostia and from there, take a ship to join her this very night, and I intended never to look back.

The Emperor dismissed me with his usual flick of a wrist, and continued to bend the ear of the young slave boy sitting at his feet about how wonderful his performance had been. I slipped out. But as I scurried away under the curvature of the theatre's walls, I felt a shadow slip past me, and a wind from nowhere blew tendrils of hair into my face.

"Run, little dream-woman," said a whisper that seemed to come from the stones of the theatre itself. "Run far away, run before the flames and the ghosts, run from the cries of the crucified and the roaring of the wild beasts; run from this city of chaos, and from the monster that rules it." Out of the corner of my eye, I saw a woman in a blood-stained blue dress walking purposefully towards the Imperial dressing-rooms.

I ran.

FINIS

AUTHOR'S NOTES

All the stories in this book except 'Dies Irae' were originally told on my podcast, *Creepy Classics*. Each episode features a discussion of various historical aspects of the story following the reading of the story itself, so for lots of detail on all sorts of aspects of these stories, check out *Creepy Classics* wherever you listen to podcasts!

Every story is inspired by a real ancient Roman ghost story – some fictional, told in poems or novels, and some as part of Roman ghost folklore, appearing his histories and letters. You can read most of the texts in English translation for free at one of two websites:

Perseus Collection, Greek and Roman materials: https://www.perseus.tufts.edu/hopper/collection?collection=Perseus:collection:Greco-Roman

Poetry in Translation: https://www.poetryintranslation.com/

The exceptions are Pliny the Younger's *Letters*, which is available to buy translated by Betty Radice and published by Penguin Classics; Valerius Maximus' *Memorable Deeds and Sayings*, which is available translated by Henry John Walker and published by Hackett Publishing Company, and Phlegon of Tralles' *Book of Marvels*, which is available translated by William Hansen and published by University of Exeter Press.

One Cheap Summer Sandal (inspired by Cicero, *On Divination*, 1.57 and Valerius Maximus, *Memorable Deeds and Sayings*, 1.7ext.10)

Cicero describes this story as "well known" when he tells it in his text on divination, and it is almost identical as told by Valerius Maximus several decades later, so it was probably a popular folktale in ancient Rome (and Valerius Maximus may have used Cicero as his source). Each author told the story for quite different reasons. Cicero includes it in a philosophical dialogue in which he has his brother Quintus put forward a series of arguments for why he should believe in divination, before having himself refute every single one of them. This is one of Quintus' stories, so it is only included so it can be disproven. Valerius Maximus, on the other hand, included it in a section of his resource book for public speakers on examples of prodigies and miracles, so he was using it to prove the efficacy of divination.

What both authors have in common, is that this is a story about divination and prophecy, and about prophetic dreams. The ghost is just the mechanism for the transmission of information the friend who is safe could not possibly know. It doesn't even matter for the telling of this story whether it is actually the soul of the dead friend who is communicating through the dream, or whether it is a god or spirit appearing as the dead friend – the prophecy is the key part.

Read more:

Juliette Harrisson, *Dreams and Dreaming in the Roman Empire: Cultural Memory and Imagination* (2013, Bloomsbury).

The Haunted House (inspired by Pliny, *Letters*, 7.27.5-11)

Pliny the Younger opens this letter to his friend Licinius Sura by asking whether he thinks ghosts exist, and then goes on to tell three stories he thinks prove that they do; this is the second. Pliny's is the oldest surviving version of this story, but very similar stories are told by Lucian (*Philopseudes*, 30-1), Constantius of Lyon (*Life of St Germanus*, 2.10), and Gregory the Great (*Dialogues*, 3.4.1-3) as well as several later authors. Pliny just says the incident took place 'in Athens', so I have based the location roughly on the Venizelos Mansion, the oldest house in Athens (which was built in the 16th century, and renovated in the 18th century). I have combined it with my own (slightly dim!) memories of being taken on a moonlit walk around the Acropolis in 2014 by my colleague Persephone Sextou while on a field trip.

Every version of the story has a different protagonist, but it is always either a philosopher (for pagans) or a bishop (for later Christians). There are at least three known philosophers called Athenodorus, all Stoics; Athenodorus of Soli, who lived in the mid-3rd century BCE, Athenodorus of Canana, who taught the young Octavian (the future Emperor Augustus), and Athendorus Cordylion, keeper of the library at Pergamon. Pliny does not give any real indication of which one he means, and Yelena Baraz has pointed out that only Athenodorus of Soli has a connection to Athens. I have been deliberately vague, as Pliny was, but implied by the reference to where the Roman Agora is "now", that it was Athenodorus of Soli, though I've had to give him a work in progress attributed to Athendororus of Canana because we do not know details of any works of the other two. I have also included a paraphrase of a famous quotation from Seneca the Younger from *Moral Letters to Lucilius*, 13.4, and some other paraphrased bits and pieces from the same letter as well. Seneca lived long after any of the Athenodorus's, but before Pliny, so it's only cheating a little bit!

Read more:

D. Felton, *Haunted Greece and Rome: Ghost Stories from Classical Antiquity* (1999, University of Texas Press).

Under the Kitchen Floor (inspired by Plautus, *Mostellaria*, 446-531)

This is the oldest story in this book, inspired by a comic play from the second century BCE, which was itself inspired by a Greek original. The most important thing about this story is that Tranio is making it up on the spot, so the ghost story is not supposed to make sense. My old man is a little braver and less gullible than Plautus's, partly because of the changes I made in abbreviating the story. I also added details from other stories – you'll recognise the ghost's charred fingers from 'A Warning' (inspired by Propertius) and the chains from 'The Haunted House' (inspired by Pliny the Younger). Maccius the real ghost is entirely my addition because I personally do not usually enjoy ghost stories that do not have a real ghost in them, and I gave him Plautus' own family name.

Read more:

Daniel Ogden, *Magic, Witchcraft and Ghosts in the Greek and Roman Worlds: A Sourcebook* (2009, Oxford University Press).

The Dead Marriage (inspired by Apuleius, *Metamorphoses* – sometimes known as *The Golden Ass* – 9.29-31)

Apuleius' *Metamorphoses*, sometimes known as *The Golden Ass* (to distinguish it from Ovid's *Metamorphoses*), is my favourite ancient novel; a rollicking ride through Greece with a man who foolishly tried to perform a witch's spell and accidentally turned himself into a donkey. Underneath the fun and silliness lies a deeply serious take on Platonic philosophy and a description of the mystery cult of the Egyptian goddess Isis that has historians battling over whether we should take it seriously or not (my answer – it's a little bit of both).

The novel is quite episodic and it spends a fair bit of time on the miller and his wife, providing lots of detail on their very bad relationship, and taking lots of tangents. I left out some sections because they were irrelevant to the story I was telling, and some because they were too unpleasant and not the sort of fiction I personally want to write (primarily, I summarised the incident with the wife's young lover rather than writing it in detail). Although the use of magic is clearly implied, I added the scene at the witch's hovel, based on several Latin poems about witches as well as my own imagination. Since the protagonist of the novel is, at this point, a donkey who has been sold to the miller, I replaced him with a human slave of the same name. The description of the horrific conditions in the mill is taken almost directly from the novel.

Read more:

Lucius Apuleius (translated by H. E. Butler), *The Apologia and Florida of Apuleius of Madaura* (1909, Dodo Press).

A Warning (re-told from Propertius, *Elegies*, 4.7 and 4.8)

I have described this story, as well as 'The Witch of Thessaly,' as "re-told" rather than "inspired by" because my narrative is very close to Propertius' original, and much of the poetry in the story is his. Propertius' two poems about his girlfriend Cynthia's death are famously listed in the "wrong" order in his collection, with her ghost appearing to tell him off in 4.7 before we read about the argument she had with Lygdamus in 4.8. I think Propertius has done this deliberately, to create a mystery around what has happened to Cynthia (who was alive and well when last seen in Book Three) before solving it with the next poem, so I used the flashback structure to try to replicate that in my story.

Propertius is one of several famous Latin love poets from the first century BCE, and I've used some of the mistresses' names from his contemporaries at the end of the story (Catullus' Lesbia, Tibullus' Delia, and Ovid's Corinna). How much of their work is autobiographical and how much fictional is unclear. Catullus' poems are probably at least partly autobiographical, as Lesbia was widely considered to be a pseudonym for a real women known for her love affairs, Clodia Pulchra, and there is probably some truth in Ovid's poems as well, but there is no evidence either way for Propertius. The Latin love poets all write about lovers they cannot or will not marry – married women, boys, and women like Cynthia who are socially unacceptable as wives. The Subura, where Cynthia lives, was a lower class area and red-light district.

Read more:

Juliette Harrisson (ed), *Imagining the Afterlife in the Ancient World* (2019, Routledge).

A Spanish Werewolf in Rome (inspired by Petronius, *Satyricon*, 61-62)

This is the only story that is not about a ghost, but a different type of monster, a werewolf. Ghosts and werewolves were quite closely connected in ancient folklore, especially in Greek folklore. The story as told by Petronius is intended to be funny; the *Satyricon* is a comic novel about the misadventures of an elite Roman man, Encolpius, and his teenage slave, Giton, who is also his lover.

Most of the *Satyricon* has only survived in fragments, but the biggest complete section is the part known as 'Trimalchio's Dinner.' In this part of the story, Encolpius and Giton go to a dinner party hosted by a freedman called Trimalchio. The big joke of the party is that Trimalchio is a vulgar fool who has a terrible sense of humour and does not know what he is talking about. The freedmen and freedwomen at the party are constantly mocked throughout by Encolpius as narrator and by the author as well, who may have been a courtier of the Emperor Nero.

In writing my version, I have tried to avoid replicating Petronius' inherent snobbery as much as possible, though I have kept the snobbery of Encolpius as a character, and I have also tried to incorporate some of the wit and humour where possible, though modern readers find very different things funny than Petronius' audience of upper class Roman men. The twist that Niceros himself is a werewolf is another addition of my own, for the same reason as the creation of Maccius for 'Underneath the Kitchen Floor' – I prefer my supernatural stories to have proper supernatural elements in them!

Read more:

Daniel Ogden, *The Werewolf in the Ancient World* (2021, Oxford University Press).

A Tomb for a Wedding-Bed (inspired by Phlegon of Tralles, *On Marvels*, 1)

Phlegon of Tralles was a Greek man from modern Turkey, living under Roman rule. He was a freedman of Emperor Hadrian, placing him in the second century CE. His *On Marvels* is essentially a collection of ancient folklore, and has some similarities with urban legends. Having said that, his stories tend to be set in specific times and places with named characters, which sets them apart from not only modern urban legends, but quite a bit of ancient folklore as well, like the story of the two friends at the inn that inspired 'One Cheap Summer Sandal.'

In my version of the story, I've played with the events slightly to speed the story up a bit and have it take place over a short period of time. I have also added some details around tokens given by Machetes and Philinnion to each other to highlight the similarities between this story and the modern urban legend of the Vanishing Hitchhiker. Although Philinnion does not stand by the roadside trying to hitch a ride, she has a lot of similarities with modern vanishing hitchhiker stories, as she is a young woman who died when on the brink of marriage and adulthood (which would make her about 12 to 15 years old in the Roman period – I aged her up to at least her late teens!) and who reappears looking for love.

Read more:

Michael Goss, *The Evidence for Phantom Hitchhikers* (2015 [1984], Coronet).

The Witch of Thessaly (re-told from Lucan, *Civil War*, 6.413-830)

Lucan (Marcus Annaeus Lucanus) lived 39-65 CE; he was forced to suicide aged 25 for conspiring against the Emperor Nero. The two had been friends, but they seem to have fallen out over poetry, at which point Lucan joined a conspiracy headed by Gaius Calpurnius Piso, ratted on his own mother, and then died. He is described in Tacitus' *Annals* and in an obscure *Life of Lucan* by Suetonius. The *Civil War*, which is sometimes called the *Pharsalia* (to distinguish it from Julius Caesar's *Civil Wars*), is an epic poem about the civil war between Julius Caesar and Pompey. This was an unusual subject for an ancient epic poem – many of them are about wars, but they usually tell mythological stories from the distant past, rather than histories only about one hundred years old. The scene in which Erichtho the witch raises a corpse to prophesy for Sextus Pompey was the focus of my Masters dissertation, many years ago.

My re-telling of this story is very close indeed to Lucan's poem, though I did cut down the description of Thessalian witches a bit and pulled back on some of the really gory stuff, simply for the sake of my own personal taste! I also left out a few of the more unpleasant ingredients for the spell. Lucan has Erichtho perform another spell in order to give the ghost the knowledge to give to Sextus, which seems entirely pointless and designed just to allow him to revel in his description of the witch a bit more. The whole idea behind raising a corpse from the dead to tell someone their future is that the dead have access to divine knowledge that the living do not. If the witch could do a spell to gain that knowledge, she could just do that, without bothering with the corpse (though Erichtho does seem the type to raise a corpse just for the fun of it).

Read more:

Daniel Ogden, *Greek and Roman Necromancy* (2001, Princeton University Press).

The Fault In Ourselves (inspired by Plutarch, *Brutus*, 36 and 48 and *Caesar*, 69)

The assassination of Julius Caesar was a frequently described event in ancient literature, so I've drawn on several other sources besides Plutarch in my description of it here, especially Suetonius' biography *Divine Julius*. I've also heavily implied that Brutus might have been Caesar's biological son, which has been rumoured since ancient times. Some historians think the timing is not right because Caesar would have been 15 years old, but since Brutus' mother Servilia, although married, was 15 years old when she had Brutus it is certainly not impossible. They almost certainly did have an affair later in their lives.

The story also incorporates Caesar's famous last words according to Suetonius, "*kai su, teknon?*" which is Greek for "And you, child." Various theories have been put forward as to why Caesar might have said this. Shakespeare changed the line to "And you, Brutus?" in Latin ("*Et tu, Brute?*") implying that Caesar was horrified at Brutus' participation because Brutus was his son. Other theories suggest it might have been a quote from a lost Greek text, since Caesar's first language would have been Latin though he would have been fluent in Greek as well, or that it was a curse, or the first part of a proverb.

Shakespeare also changed the nature of the spirit that appeared to Brutus in his tent before the battle of Philippi, making it Caesar's ghost. But all the ancient sources agree that it was Brutus' own "*daimōn kakos*", "bad spirit." I've combined the two by having it shift between looking like Brutus and looking like Caesar!

Read more:

Kathryn Tempest, *Brutus: The Noble Conspirator* (2017, Yale University Press).

Of Blood And Gods (inspired by Suetonius, *Augustus*, 6)

Both this and the following story are almost entirely my own invention, based on a few lines of text! Suetonius briefly explains that a room identified by locals as the Emperor Augustus' nursery is haunted, and that the new owner was flung out of bed and found wrapped in sheets by the door the next morning. I expanded this to be a story about Augustus himself, going right back to his childhood but providing a parade of the people he will hurt or kill as a ruthless Emperor as an adult, a sort of reversal of the famous parade of great Romans from Virgil's *Aeneid*.

I also had to deal with the fact that Augustus has more names than a character in a Russian novel; he was born Gaius Octavius, named after his father; then according to Suetonius he was nicknamed Thurinus when he was young; then after Julius Caesar posthumously adopted him in his will he became Gaius Julius Caesar Octavianus, usually shortened to Octavian by historians, then finally he took the name Augustus in 27

BCE, re-naming himself to mark his new regime and separate himself from the hundreds of people he had killed or who died in battle in the process of him making himself Emperor.

Augustus' biological father is not usually talked about much compared to Julius Caesar, but Suetonius says Octavius was late to hear the conspiracy of Catiline brought before the Senate because Atia was in labour, so I have assumed from this that he was a reasonably affectionate and involved father! Other details of Augustus' birth are invented from my own personal experience and general knowledge of childbirth; the mother telling everyone it's not happening and she's going home is something that sometimes happens during childbirth. The location of Augustus' birth was debated already in the first century CE. Suetonius records the birthplace of Augustus as at the Ox-Heads in the Palatine and says there was a shrine there; but he also says that near Velitrae the locals think he was born in this nursery in his grandfather's house, so that is where I have placed it.

Read more:

P. G. Maxwell-Stuart, *Poltergeists: A History of Violent Ghostly Phenomena* (2011, Amberley).

Home (inspired by Tacitus, *Annals*, 11.20-21 and Pliny the Younger, *Letters*, 7.27)

This story is also spun out from a few lines in Pliny's letter. It was difficult to write because it's a long way out of my own experience, and based on a story told by ancient Romans, who are not exactly known for their sensitivity to topics relating to human diversity. I sincerely hope the story as I have written is not insulting to anyone – it is certainly not intended to be so!

Neither Tacitus nor Pliny describe the skin colour of either Curtius Rufus or the "spirit of Africa" at all. I have based my description of the spirit loosely on Shelley P. Haley's translation of an Augustan poem called *Moretum*, and assumed

Rufus to have a brown skin tone similar to a well known portrait of the North African Emperor Septimius Severus. Tacitus reports the rumour that Curtius Rufus was the son of a gladiator, and one possibility is that his mother had an affair; Juvenal (writing several decades later) makes snide remarks in his poem *Satire 6* about women having affairs with gladiators and, separately, about women getting abortions to avoid giving birth to 'Aethiopian' babies. Alternatively, he might have been adopted by the Curtii, but the level of the scandal maybe suggests his mother having an affair (whether or not it was with a gladiator) is more likely. The Curtius Rufus described by Tacitus and Pliny may or may not be the same writer as an historian who wrote a history of Alexander the Great, Quintus Curtius Rufus.

The drunken Hercules is a description of a small statue I saw in the Bardo Museum in Tunis in 2008, and 'Nasidienus' is from Martial's *Epigrams*. The amphitheatre at El Jem (Thysdrus) was actually built a couple of centuries later, but there may have been an earlier one on the site!

Read more:

Shelley P. Haley's chapter 'Black Feminist Thought and Classics: Re-membering, Re-claiming, Re-empowering,' in Nancy Sorkin Rabinowitz and Amy Richlin (eds), *Feminist Theory and the Classics* (1993, Routledge).

A Tortured Soul (inspired by Suetonius, *Caligula*, 59)

Suetonius' set of biographies of *Twelve Caesars* tells several ghost stories relating to Emperors and is a major source for this book, as you might imagine! It's not surprising that there were ghost stories around Caligula, considering his mental difficulties in life, his violent death, and the fact that his cremation was rushed and not properly finished. Improperly buried people coming back as ghosts is an extraordinarily common theme in ancient ghost stories, and has already been seen in 'The Haunted House.'

Suetonius says that Caligula was killed in a covered corridor and that there were terrors every night in the *domus* (house) where he was killed until it was destroyed by fire. I've interpreted this as being the Great Fire of Rome of 64 CE, during the reign of Nero, though there were a couple of great fires and a lot of smaller fires in Rome, so it may not have been that specific fire. As I was writing the story, I also suddenly realized I needed to know who buried him, which none of the historians have specified. Herod Agrippa or Caligula's freedmen (former slaves freed by him who, according to Roman social rules, owed him continued work and loyalty). Narcissus was one of Claudius' freedmen who helped him rule as Emperor, so I've assumed he was freed after helping on this day.

Read more:

Charles W. King, *The Ancient Roman Afterlife: Di Manes, Belief, and the Cult of the Dead* (2020, University of Texas Press).

Dies Irae (inspired by Suetonius, *Nero*, 34)

I have been struggling with how to approach the story of Agrippina's ghost for years! Nero was a deeply unpleasant person who murdered most of his female relatives, in one case personally (rather than by ordering her death as Emperor). Since I do not personally want to write about domestic violence, that makes him a difficult character for me to cover. It was also another story which required me to expand on a fairly short section of the ancient text. I went through several different ideas, including telling the story from the point of view of one of Nero's slaves, and telling it from Agrippina's own point of view and having her turn into a Fury in the underworld, werewolf-transformation-style.

In the end, I settled on the point of view of a professional dream interpreter called on by Nero to sort out his bad dreams. This allowed me to explore the characters from the outside, and have my protagonist be a more down to earth ancient Roman. I toyed with whether they should be a man or a woman. The surviving dream interpretation book from the Roman world, written in Greek in the second century CE, was written by a man called Artemidorus. However, in Martial's *Epigram* 7.54, when the poet is complaining that his friend Nasidienus keeps dreaming about him, he says he has been to the *saga*, which could be translated as wise-woman, female soothsayer, or witch, to counter Nasidienus' dreams' effects. In the end I split the difference and made my dream interpreter a woman who, like many female writers of the 19th century later would, wrote under a male name.

Read more:

Emma Southon, *Agrippina: The Defiant Story of Rome's First Empress* (2024 [2018], Unbound).

ABOUT THE AUTHOR

Juliette Harrisson is a writer, historian, Trekkie, and cat-lady-turned-dog-person. Her original specialism was myth and religion in the ancient Roman world, but she's since branched out to explore myth, legend, folklore, ghost stories, witchcraft, and weird and wonderful history in general from all over time and space. She's published numerous chapters, two edited volumes, and one monograph, but this is her first fiction book.

Juliette lives in England and spends her free time dog-walking and toddler-wrangling.

https://jgharrisson.wordpress.com/

YouTube: @ClassicalJG
TikTok: @classicaljg
Instagram: @classicaljgh

Made in United States
Troutdale, OR
03/23/2025